MW00779854

BREATH WARMTH & DREAM

THE KHUMALO TRILOGY **BOOK ONE**

ZIG ZAG CLAYBOURNE

BREATH, WARMTH, & DREAM

Copyright © 2024 by Clarence Young

All rights reserved.

This is a work of fiction. Characters, events, and organizations portrayed in this novel are products of the author's imagination or are used fictitiously.

Obsidian Sky Books
Detroit, MI

ISBN 978-1-7322980-3-3

First Edition: April 2024

Cover art and interior design by
Jesse Hayes, anansihayes.com

For Jasmine and Zariah
and
with blessings toward Bea and the girls

PART ONE

NOT A TOAST

The sun, as welcome on the back of the old man's neck as a hot knife, sliced him as he told the unconscious woman, "In raising this cup to your lips, I bind you to me."

The mage's voice was as coarse as pebbles under a toe, his mannerisms and clothing tight as a too-small boot. He lost a mottled boiled-cabbage hand inside colorful scarves while raising the woman's wrapped head and parched lips toward a hammered tin cup. His thin arm braced her with difficulty yet care. It wouldn't do for a single drop of enchanted water to make its way to the earth.

Twitswaddle had never tried an energy binding on someone from foreign soil; in truth, he'd never have considered any of the travelers amidst the mercantile grounds established along the coast, but times were lean and he'd sensed this one's passage from across two stalls as though she'd brushed against him. He'd studied her for days to make sure she was prey he could handle. Here, though, in a deserted patch of road along the woods far from any bustle, and under a sun far too insistent, he felt the sure power inside her frame and the imaginative energies within her skull, and wondered—very quickly, so that he could easily dismiss it—had he misjudged that ability to handle?

The charcoal skin against his palm was soft and warm from lying under a cloudless sky.

Her lips: severe and slightly parted. Her eyes...

She opened her eyes.

Chosen prey never opened their eyes. The drugs he employed ensured they remained inert until the binding of their energy to his life.

"I suspected," she said, "it was you." Even stern and accusatory, her voice had a musical quality. Her words felt physical.

Theophilus Twitswaddle froze.

"I am, however," she continued, content to allow his now-very-quaking arm to hold her at the level at which they might easily speak as she looked upward into his rheumy eyes, "thirsty." She gave a commanding tilt of her chin to the ugly metal cup with many lightning bolts inexpertly hammered across it.

He tipped the cup to her lips, the entire enterprise now unsure, while remembering to recite again as she drank, his tone tremulous rather than confident. "I...bind you to me."

Mother Khumalo drank, dabbed her mouth with the back of a hand, and said, "I think not." She sat immediately upright. He nearly fell, fumbling to retrieve something from an inner pocket of his ridiculously tight vest. "The wand you are reaching for?" She held a length of gnarly twig. "Simple theft. The fact that you cannot speak is my breath in your throat." She laid a hand against his startled, mottled face, gently, allowing his cheek to contour to her palm. "In a few moments, you will not be able to move. That is the poison now entering your flesh. If you panic, you endanger yourself. Otherwise, my breath in your throat will keep you breathing. Do you understand?" Khumalo watched his thieving eyes for answer. They quickly centered, steadied, and waited. "Good." She rolled to her knees. Since the thief mage couldn't move, she arranged him a bit more comfortably, then tended to her own comfort, sitting back to tuck her many-colored robe's hem into the hollow of her slender, crossed legs. She leaned forward, resting her forearms casually atop her knees.

"You're about the age I expected you to be," she said, her Afrelan accent shaping syllables into lilting notes. "It takes a certain dissatisfaction gained over time to believe you are owed what is not remotely yours. You are a reverse spider, drying prey to husks, then feeding on their renewal. How many have you used this dehydration spell on, coupled with dreary sleeps? I'm sure far more than the three bodies dead of desiccation over the course of my time here. Having people come to their great mage for advice was brilliant; calling a general assembly on the docks to announce efforts to rout the villain, I give you marks for that. When you answered the young lady's question on what you would do toward those ends, you said, 'I will sleep on that,' with all due gravitas and, unfortunately, the most minute measure of being pleased with yourself to prick my ears. I'm only here in your lovely coastal village awaiting my daughter who's gone sailing. She arrives in two more days. That allows plenty of time for you to satisfy my curiosity."

Mother Khumalo inspected the wand. Its wood wanted to tell her everything the thief mage had made it do. Mostly, it needed rest, solitude, and peace of mind. With her free hand, she pushed a portion of air out of sync with the air around it until a pocket was made of nothingness. She slid the wand into the pocket, then, with proper effort, continued pushing until her arm disappeared to the elbow.

When she pulled back, the arm and hand emerged unscathed. The wand remained inside.

The mage's rapt eyes ricocheted between the air healing itself, Khumalo's hands, and her placid expression betrayed solely by the tiniest satisfied raising of a brow.

"I could put you there as well, but you wouldn't fare the better," she said. "The question then becomes what to do with you. The answer is simple, Twitswaddle: I make you a promise that if you are ever trouble again, I will be the least of your problems. I will unleash my daughter on you and she will devour you from the inside out, soul to bone to hair to skin, until even memories of you in others' minds are gone. Amnandi Khumalo is known as the Beast of the World. Were you more than a fortunate charlatan, you'd know that." She leaned forward a bit more to lance him with her eyes, hoping not to show the true image her mind held of her daughter, a studious, mischievous, caring child of huge promise. "Do you accept my words, Mr. Twitswaddle?"

She knew from his panicked eyes he was trying to nod.

"I'm glad we found this common ground." Mother Khumalo stood in one easy, fluid motion, briefly obscuring his view behind a swirl of reds, yellows, and greens in a combination of silks and heavier fabrics. Then the sun returned, bright in the midday sky. "There's a chance my magicks might be permanent. You'll know after a day." She searched him, removing all useful accoutrements from his person, be they magical or practical, then rolled him to his back, arranging his body in a passable sleeper's position. "You are responsible for three deaths that I know of. The beasts in the woods will not eat you, but the scent of my magicks on you might attract other things. May you cause less suffering in your next life."

With two pockets of jangling magics and baubles, Mother Khumalo left the Thief Mage Theophilus Twitswaddle on the dry, barren, baking ground to eventually present her full findings and statement to the local constabulary. She found his horse in a wood some ways away from the dusty road and released it, leaving the saddle for whoever had need. It was a good day for another long walk, and the sun was no bother.

***

Where so many considered the bustle and promise of new goods excitements in themselves, the only time a port held any anticipation for her was if she was meeting someone. Ayanda Khumalo spoke to spirits and rode—on occasion—the winds. Bustle and baubles in and of themselves were useless unless viewed as connected to the life forces which created them.

The one life force in the world that excited her beyond measure was due to arrive at the tip of a wind which Khumalo refrained from requesting move faster. She did, however, strain her essence outward to sense the ship's approach, felt as a tittering joy between the hull's wood and the sea's happy spray. She reined herself in and rested an arm comfortably atop a wharf post. The wind toyed with her loose scarves and comfortable robe. Not brusquely. Companionably. Khumalo settled on appreciating the sun, air, and waves for the hour it would take the old ship to reach Waterfall's shallows, waves which slapped the massive pylons below in an unending bid for rightful attention. The rhythm was soothing. No one bothered Khumalo, no one spoke to her— meaning she found each moment's passage blissful.

People sold things along the wharf, but she barely noticed. Pleasure seekers and pleasure givers, out at all times of the day, exchanged intentions, often laughing at the joy of the sudden fortune in finding one another across a world of pains and obligations. Khumalo couldn't help loosing a tiny smile herself, even though her eyes never left the water. People who enjoyed themselves with such abandon gave off a scent akin to flowers, not that they themselves could smell it, but to a witch's nose it was a perfume of surprising delight among the more muted, banal windsprints of human life.

She also noticed, without taking her eyes from the sea, when she was noticed. Ayanda Khumalo stood a head taller than almost everyone in this "new world" south of Afrela even though there wasn't a new world on the globe of Erah beneath anyone's feet. Her scarves and robes were always brightly colored, always immaculate, always arranged just so, and she had a habit of humming (often without being aware of it) in highly varying pitches like bees convening sudden meetings, which, taken as a whole, drew attention from even the dullest observer. Although her peoples traveled everywhere, this new world had elevated foolish men from farmers to kings to gods, bringing all manner of problems. The dark shine of her skin sometimes drew glances. Glances were ignored; foolishness was not.

Very few indulged their foolishness around Ayanda Khumalo. Those who did were usually of the sort as the idiot mage, hungry for a soul of their own. Whether the constabulary found him or he exiled himself wasn't a concern right now. There'd be no more unexplained deaths to add to the vague dourness she felt from this place. Unhappiness was like a cork pulled from a barrel, letting all manner of spirit and joy leak out. There were so many unhappy people, however, she received no impression of such dispiritedness around her now—which was good. The mossy taste of the barely felt spray slowly coating the line of her mouth was excellent. It reminded her of her own coastal upbringing. The plan had been to sail the world for the fun of it—which meant education, the pinnacle of fun—and return when Amnandi was ready to establish a home of her own. The two of them had traveled from the Motherland's beautiful shores to cold Strasic, from there a year in mountain lands, then months among the temples of Shau, and a long sail to this "new world" called Eurola, although it had been established for centuries. Some called Eurola "Patch." As in *dirt patch*. At times, they even called it this without spitting in the general direction of the holdings of the wealthier among them, an act Khumalo found strange and distasteful. Everything here seemed built on transactions meant to weaken the weak while building up all others. It was odd, sometimes interesting, but Khumalo intrinsically knew Eurola, and this part of it, the commerce port of Waterfall, was a good place to visit, but she would not want to stay, not unless she could find a space untouched by a conglomerate of quiet desperations. She hadn't visited a single spot in Eurola where clouds of individual need hadn't hung in the air like reverse pollen, deadening dreams and stifling growth, very different from the communal aesthetic of Insheree, her home city. Even the magick here was different. In her mind, Eurolan magick was "magic"—lacking the weight of her language's harder, respectful edge to the word. *Magic* was too often meant to take something, very rarely to give.

Magick, however...

From the corner of her eye she noted an elder approaching her. It was a beggar she had spoken with many times along this wharf. Her name was Orsys.

By now, the ship was quite nearer.

Orsys took up position a few feet from Khumalo's pylon. Her voice, rarely used, erupted rough and staccato. "You've been waiting a while. Who is he, then?"

"We haven't spoken of romances, you and I. Why am I waiting for 'him'?"

"Woman, then. Pack mule. I don't care. Have you coin?"

"I do."

"Can I have some?"

Khumalo left the sea to respect the elder's gaze. Orsys was a bundle of strips salvaged from at least a dozen different pieces of clothing, none ragged and all expertly stitched, certainly not by her unsteady hands, but Elder Orsys never spoke of her benefactors, of which she clearly had several. Her gray pigtails were never unkempt; she walked with a stoop and with pain out of age, not from nights on the ground; she'd been portly in her prime, yet her skin sagged mainly from gravity's long embrace, not sudden weight loss. Orsys received shelter, care, and cleaning from a number of sources—this Khumalo knew from the varying angle of her back from varying mattresses—but Orsys saw no need as yet to speak of anything beyond the immediate on those occasions she ambled up to Khumalo.

"I can give you all," said Khumalo. She always responded thusly.

"Too much frightens me. I only need enough." The elder always responded thusly, rhythmically tapping fingers against the tips of the other hand to calm herself as she did so. It was a good exercise, bringing a sharpness to her eyes the longer she conversed.

Khumalo pulled a pouch from an inside chest pocket and proffered two large worn coins of stamped bronze bearing the sigil of whoever called himself king there at the moment. It was a silly use of metal that could have gone toward building something.

"May enough be your blessing."

Orsys held a blue pocket open as wide as possible on her red, blue, and brown wrap.

Khumalo dropped the coins while the elder, exhibiting the smallest vestige of pride, looked quickly away to the sea.

A pat to the pocket from Orsys to flatten it returned her wizened eyes upward to Khumalo.

"You're so tall," Orsys remarked.

"Do you like that?" Khumalo said kindly.

"I do." When Orsys smiled, every wrinkle on her sun-bleached face moved like sudden lightning flashes, brightening the old woman's visage immeasurably.

"How many people have come off ships hoping to see your smile, dear one?" said Khumalo.

"My husband studied fish! My second husband traded...things; I don't remember what. He took my daughter with him on short trips. She always bounced off the boats with a new pelt cap from wherever the gods sent them. Always. Will your lover have a cap?"

"Are you aware of what *living vicariously* means?"

Orsys nodded excitedly.

"And you're fine with receiving such life through me?"

Orsys nodded vigorously.

"I'm waiting for my daughter."

Orsys thrilled so suddenly, she did something she rarely did: touched someone. She grasped Khumalo's hand in a pleased squeeze so quickly she likely didn't realize it herself, and let go just as quickly, just as unaware.

"We have daughters!" the old woman said, eyes wide open to show the blue still in them. "Mine sailed away."

Khumalo smiled. "We do. Mine is on a similar errand with a friend I've met here."

"Not a lover?"

"No."

"A friend."

"Yes."

"Friends are good."

"They are."

"But only if you trust them."

"Is there a definition of *friend* I'm unfamiliar with?"

"No. Her name, tell me her name."

What a wonderful woman. It would have been good to get to know her fully at some point, but there was likely not to be time for that. Two things did not stop: the progression of age, and Khumalo's determination to see as much of the world for as long as she could. "Amnandi. It means *sweet*."

"I like that. May I stay here to meet her?"

"Yes." Khumalo suspected the elder would wander long before that, but to have her beside her in silence was no hardship. There were enough waves for both to think upon and sufficient time in which to do it.

THE SHIP

All ten years of Amnandi Khumalo ran like the wind around the crowded ship, the quickest, most wide-eyed "Beast of the World" (a nickname her mother used only when tickling her before initiating a game of chase) the crew of the *Bane* had ever seen. During her time on board, she had learned to tie knots, set posts, manage sails, and (most importantly) keep out of the way when need of that particular skill arose.

Her zipping now was for the best places to watch. The crow's nest was forbidden to her; the current pilot at the pilot's station hadn't taken the crew's liking to her, and so many were already gathered at the prow, she expected the captain's melodious voice to order everyone away at any moment, but seeing home after any voyage was exciting, especially when the rewards of the trip were varied and bountiful.

She found a spot between two betrothed sailors, ragged men

who both smelled of salt and sawdust from working in ship's carpentry all the time (another of her favorite places). She loved the spray peppering her face as she hefted herself up on the knotty railing, tiptoes lifting her on deck. Sarantain and Grucca inched apart, knowing the girl liked her space.

Of all the things Amnandi adored about being on the water, the feeling of the wind was her favorite. Land wind felt as though it had rules constraining it. Water wind was as wild as hopping through portals during a game of chase, something she had gotten exceedingly good at.

"*A witch,*" her mother would say, "*is powerful on land but communes with the goddess when at sea. Speak kindly should you see her.*"

Mother was on land somewhere along that distant mass. Mother had a saying for everything.

Amnandi appreciated each one.

She was glad no one on board treated her like this voyage was her first time on water. She'd sailed before, yet this was different from a passenger ship and, most excitingly, she was alone. Even between these two big men, she was alone.

Until a huge shadow crept over her.

"Have you spotted her?" said a stone-smoothed voice behind her, his presence edging the two sailors even farther to accommodate him out of respect and admiration. Everyone had seen how well he protected Amnandi. Their judgments upon him were thus favorable, even though he was an outsider.

He waited patiently for her to answer in case she was off in one of her other minds, but no, she turned her bright, dark face immediately to him and shook her head.

He pulled his scope from his hip holster and set a small crate before her. Merchant ships, thank the gods, weren't made for children as crew.

She stepped atop the crate and accepted the scope in the same motion.

This land had a condensed quality to its spirit. Every part of it Amnandi and her mother had thus traveled was a small world contained within itself, not only geographically but of the people themselves. Colonies tethered to some greater land. Mother said such communities were always designed to fail because they were viewed as adjuncts, not familial extensions regardless of their makeup. The goddess gave the world great connected bodies of water in hopes her fledglings would see how lovely the link was, not how ripe the profits.

Greens to Amnandi's left: forests. Gray and brown to her right: villages stretching toward rocky heights. An adjustment of the scope brought the distant harbor into view, not so close now as to make out individuals, but it quickened her young heart.

She'd enjoyed traveling alone, but Mother was home. Home on that bank—Amnandi was certain—in colorful scarves among drab grays and browns, the occasional orange, standing as strong as any anchor post along a massive wharf full of jostling boats.

Home. Waiting for her daughter to come home.

The giant behind her realigned the crate, angling her body toward the lee side of a wide inlet. "We put in there, not where we left."

"That doesn't seem sensible," she said, then decided, "Boats move around too much."

"You're too new in the world for pronouncements," the giant said. "Sarantain, do ships move too much?"

"Constantly," said Sarantain, offering the brightly-clad miniature sailor a quick wink even though she had her eye glued to her fascinating view of the world.

"They move," the giant said, tapping Amnandi once on the shoulder to have the scope returned briefly, "to be efficient. There are always more ships preparing to leave than those returning.

When it's our turn to leave again, we take their slot. Does that make sense?"

Amnandi stared upward at him a moment. Bog of Nasthra always occupied a full sky no matter her angle looking at him. She knew the archipelagos of tightly wound stubble under his chin and along his neck, was always concerned about the scar that went from collarbone to behind his right ear. Bog was not the largest person she'd ever seen, but he had what her mother would call "weight." Certain people, Mother Khumalo had advised Amnandi to notice, moved through the world with a weight upon them invisible to all but sensed by those versed in compassion.

"A witch enters no space dispassionately."

The young one nodded at Bog. Things moved when they needed to. She was well acquainted with that.

Having seen what he needed—that the coastline remained calm—Bog returned the scope to her. "I have to see to other duties," he said. He gave a tight nod to Grucca and Sarantain with a tilt of his eyes toward Amnandi. They returned the nod in kind. "Does this seem like a good spot to you?" Bog asked her.

"It seems like the best. I'll be here."

"Good." Bog left her to the spray, the sky, and all the gulls above.

***

All ten years of her found another best, because somehow, she made it to the prow of the ship despite the deep press of bodies waving hands, caps, or tools at those ashore. The return of family, even after a two-week voyage, was often the only cause for celebration available during daily life. The wharf was by no means thronged, but those present—provided they kept out of the way of those actually working the harbor and goods—enlivened returns to keep sailors motivated to go out again.

Amnandi perched atop Grucca's shoulders. Everyone knew Bog would have found her, just as Bog knew Grucca and Sarantain would have found him if need arose. Never had so many subtly cared for one so small at sea, owing mainly to Amnandi's unswerving willingness to help—and help well—at any suitable task (although partly to having zero desire to anger the mother in the slightest).

Bog waded through the press easily. "Have you spotted her?"

Amnandi, actually taller than him for once, passed the scope and pointed.

Bog sighted. Mother Ayanda Khumalo gave the appearance of a nebula at sunset, nothing but colors in human form. He tweaked the sight. In focus, she was the human form allowed to play as the universe. Tall she was, as people from the northern coasts of Afrela often were, as tall as he himself, and he'd never seen a sharper set of eyes. He imagined she saw his eye through the burnished tube, watching her. Somehow, on that wharf, she wasn't looking in the general direction of the ship; she looked at *them*. No one stood within several paces on either side of her. He'd noticed she traveled within a bubble of intentional solitude.

Perhaps that was where the sense of grace came from. The eyes were sharp but as serene as certain memories. They saw everything. She reminded him very much of dawn fog over a stream. He had been honored to play chaperone to her daughter.

"Gather your satchels," he told Amnandi. "When we depart, you ride my shoulders as befits a queen." Plus, the easier to keep track of her.

"Meet here?" she asked.

"I'm rooted as an old tree."

Grucca lowered her. Grucca looked exactly like his name sounded: a weathered tree whose trunk laughed at axes. She thanked him, then darted expertly among the bustle, quickly out of Bog's sight.

Grucca knew Bog as *Bog the Unsmiling* but was not a person to assume anyone was any single thing. He and Bog were roughly the same age and build, roughly the same shade of well-lived tree bark, yet not once had Grucca thought to challenge Bog. Grucca knew that he, Grucca, would lose, for the first, and for the second, violence wasn't fit for pointless games. Fist, sword, or bow were sport for the foolish. Benben Grucca didn't entertain fools.

Bog the Protector suited the scarred, quiet poet beside him. A worthy title whether Grucca spoke it aloud or not.

"Was this journey worthwhile for you?" Grucca asked Bog.

"My purse is filled. I've breathed. I've worked."

Grucca nodded approvingly. "If we're ever to sail again together, I welcome it."

"As do I."

WARMTH

"**U**nina!" The little one waved from Bog's shoulders to her smiling mother as the big man walked along the wharf.

Mother Khumalo raised a hand, the effect being people who had unconsciously crowded nearer equally unconsciously edged away. Mother paid them no mind. The Beast of the World grinned at her, nothing but teeth and bright eyes. Khumalo then waited, re-plaiting her hands inside the billowy sleeves of her robe, until the giant of an escort was within range, then held her arms out, at which Amnandi immediately flew into them, the child's dropped satchel smoothly caught by Bog as though practiced.

Khumalo hugged her daughter tightly.

Orsys, still nearby, remained silent but watchful. Excessive emotion made her withdraw into herself, but the light she saw there was both bright and warm. She wanted to remember it.

"You're a head taller than when you left," Khumalo teased, eyes closed in the squeeze. "You should have carried your benefactor." Khumalo allowed her eyes to gleam Bog's way.

"Bog is heavier than the ship. Look at his arms. We should have sunk."

"But you didn't." Khumalo inclined her head at Bog. "A debt to your delicate nature."

"Body of a bull," Bog said, then tapped his sweaty forehead, "brain of a hare. Very light."

"Balance," said Khumalo.

"Balance," said Bog.

They moved along lest the press move them. Bog easily shouldered a large, worn pack tight with goods, baubles, and whatnots.

He noted the old woman following them.

They reached Khumalo's horses, fine animals, one large, one small, both with keen, intelligent ears and discerning eyes.

"Will you eat with us?" Amnandi asked Bog.

"I need a bit of rest."

"A tavern hostel is no place for rest," said Khumalo. "Stay the night with us."

"Will your shadow approve?" he said, tipping his head backwards at Orsys.

Khumalo turned to her. "I have room for you if you'd like."

"No," said Orsys.

"May *he* stay?"

Orsys nodded, then, satisfied at some private conclusion known only to herself, ambled off.

"My horse is at the far-end stables," said Bog.

"We'll wait," said Amnandi.

"Perhaps he'll need someone walking along to protect him?" said Khumalo.

Amnandi hopped astride her mount. "Natuun will protect you."

He patted the young horse's neck. "No doubt of it."

"I've told her about you."

"She approves of me?"

"She hopes she doesn't have to take you anywhere."

"Let her know if it comes to a ride, I'll carry her." He saluted his leave of Khumalo. He and Amnandi ambled as well, the child talking excitedly each step of the way.

***

Ten-year-olds don't think of themselves as children, but—as children—when they're tired and have eaten, they fall asleep. Amnandi lay peacefully on her pallet in the small structure she and her nomadic mother currently called home. Had someone grouped several outhouses together under one roof that pitched so sharply upward, it could have served as a massive arrowhead, they would have engineered a twin to this home. But it had a door, and two decent windows front and back, one of which now poured light from Erah's moon Sharda onto a sleeping, happy child. Khumalo and Amnandi rarely needed a table, but there had been a much-abused one left behind by whoever had abandoned the shack, along with splintery chairs, so it remained in the middle. There was a small cast iron stove—which Khumalo had enthusiastically cleaned and brought back to usable life—and planks set in seemingly random places along all walls as floating shelves.

Amnandi loved the pointy roof and had made a game of trying to toss things on it without them sliding off. Wreaths of flowers and balls of vines decorated grayed wooden shingles which, to Amnandi, looked like ragged fingernails.

To Khumalo it was a space with a stove, agreeable spirits, and enough room to walk the legs from one side to another. An assortment of roots, herbs, jars of what appeared to be ordinary dirt, and a set of highly colorful clay bowls—these from home in Afrela—served as décor.

Outside, Khumalo and Bog enjoyed the hum of nighttime insects alongside the rustling of animals trying to move about unnoticed.

Evening matched the hue of the tea in the earthen mugs cupped by both her and Bog. "So," said Khumalo, and, when she was sure he was alert and attentive, completed with, "Were there issues?"

"Not a one. And you?"

"Nothing of importance."

"I imagine 'nothing of importance' for you," he said, "would cause legions to faint."

"Or run."

"Especially run."

"You're a perceptive mountain, Bog of unnamed lands."

"Next to you I'm but a weathered tree."

They sat side by side, cross-legged on the grass, a clear view of a million stars and a fat moon greeting them. He nodded at the planet's great, bright cousin. "You've been there, haven't you?"

Khumalo blew into her tea for the delicious scent it offered. "Not yet."

"What peoples do you imagine are there?"

"Likely the same fools and prophets as here."

"I've had more than enough of both. Fools, prophets, and demons. If Sharda's free of them, I'll journey there."

She nudged his shoulder with her own. "You've a winged horse?"

"I'll find one."

"I imagine you would. Thank you for minding my daughter."

"Your trust honored my ancestors. I am but their sum."

"I haven't heard anyone speak that greeting since before Amnandi was born."

"I pick things up."

"You're sentimental to your core, sir," she said, and meant it.

His only answers were a slow sip of his tea and a studious fixation on the moon.

"Thank you for keeping your weapon stored."

"And you know this how?" he asked.

"She never mentioned it."

"I had other weapons."

"I know. For someone who's never had children, you're remarkably intuitive."

"I know people. She's a small people. It was a pleasure minding her."

"In that she needed very little minding."

"Exactly. I'd say she's her mother's daughter, but I don't want to presume against how interesting she is."

"You've only known me two months. I didn't want to overwhelm you," said Khumalo.

He barked a laugh and handed her his empty cup with thanks. He listened for movement within the shack. There was none. "She sleeps soundly for a child. No flatulence, snoring, or fidgeting."

"She visits other realms. It requires her body to focus."

"I had an aunt who was a witch."

"Did she die peaceably?"

"She did not," he said simply. "Nor did my father and mother. Those three were my entire family."

"Apologies," she intoned.

"You're terrible at small talk, Ayanda Khumalo."

"This is true." She thought on this a moment. "We are not

small people."

"This is true."

"The stories about you and me are much embellished," she said.

"Equally true. But even an embellished story requires a story to begin with."

"You are a traveler, a warrior, and a poet. Tell the moon a story about yourself."

"For another night. I am a barbarian. I, too, am tired and in need of dreams."

"Our home is yours."

"May I bathe first?"

"There's a tub in the back. I'll heat it while you prepare."

"The only preparation I need is to remove these aromatic rags," he said, gesturing at his body.

"In that case, I'll heat it *before* you prepare. Excuse me." She stood, disappeared behind the well-isolated shack, and returned mere moments later, touching a hand to her heart and forehead in good-night to him.

When he rounded the shack there was no sign of flint, fire, or kiln, and yet—out of curiosity—Bog dipped a hand into the two rain barrels set on their sides and halved. The water was clean, plentiful, and warm.

***

The goddess asked him three things in the dream, and because it was a dream, Bog knew to answer very carefully.

She spoke in a language that was not meant to be translated. The questions left him uneasy. They were questions about blood, death, and suffering.

He had an answer for each.

Blood was the stain covering a barbarian head to toe.

Death tended ledgers wherever he went. As for suffering, he couldn't remember the last time he had a simple pleasurable dream, a dream of walking or eating or laughing at the brilliance of silliness. Suffering and a gray dream life were one and the same.

The goddess uncoiled her black-and-gold body, loops and loops of reticulated serpentine, until the wings at her midpoint were revealed, and then those at her back. She beckoned him to climb atop her proffered palm, to walk along the lava field of her arm, so that he might speak eye to eye. He did so sure-footed, unburnt despite the heat, his pace unhurried but steady. At full stretch, the goddess could nibble the topmost leaves of the Bao Tree, the constant green tint of her lips evidence of eager partaking.

When at last he stood along her bicep to face her, her huge star-filled eyes spoke a final, fourth question to him.

What have you taken that was not yours?

"Everything I have," he answered...but there were no words. Only spirit could speak this close to the goddess. Only spirit extended like roots from his soles to join with the celestial warmth of her body.

It was an honest admission, and in that honesty, a memory.

He sent himself to Karad again, the great desert place where he had attended university. Small, he was, barely a step away from being older than Amnandi. A prodigy, it was spoken. Young Bog had brought new insights to the philosophy of the Verse and the Blade.

His adherence to truth became legendary.

This slight boy—albeit showing signs in his developing arms, legs, and back of sinew to come—traveled the university at night. Sleep had never been an easy thing for him. Night quieted his mind enough in order for his thoughts to present themselves in an orderly fashion.

The night of the first beheading, he'd been thinking about displacement. A rock thrown at water sank; a massive boat guided onto water did not. The science had been explained to him well enough; the philosophy had not.

A sudden skirmish behind a wall of bushels across the way caught his attention;

Then someone making an attempt to run;

Then two sets of hands violently halting the runner.

A foot from behind the bushels kicked hard into the back of a knee. The runner went down, still held fast.

In a motion nearly a dance, the two restrainers spun away, the kicking foot planted itself, never revealing the attacker's entire body. The flash of a perfect blade dropped as if from the moon itself, and then a head dropped.

Next the body. Followed by the running of demons, the three assailants as quiet as Bog's held breath at the corner he peered from behind, their footfalls more rapid than his heart. It had taken less than ten seconds, but the goddess saw how it formed him, and so asked again:

What have you taken that was not yours?

He learned an important lesson not taught in the blade mastery courses: murder was not clinical or clean. He spoke of that night to no one, and for a season afterward very rarely spoke beyond a cursory mumble or grunt. During the investigation, he answered official queries with something entirely new to him: lies.

"I don't know."

"I wasn't there."

"Was the man important?"

All spoken dully, as though by another person.

The last was the biggest lie. He had grown believing everyone was important. Every life seemed connected, even the lives of the countless people he'd never meet and the infinite ancestors providing each day's energy and purpose—all a part of him.

Sacred.

That lie snapped his focus as crisply as bones in a neck.

His neck at the time was thin and particularly vulnerable.

His evaluations faltered in everything but the physical arts. The sword became a shield, martial science and the physics of both giving and deflecting pain became confidantes to the child, lovers to the young man, and counselors to the huge wanderer beset by the world's ills.

He knew what this dream would require of him: blood. With the very next thought, his blade was in one hand, the axe in the other.

The goddess's golden-cracked ebony face remained impassive as she gave him his wordless mission. He turned, strode down her arm, and—in the waking world—was not aware that Ayanda Khumalo sat quietly near, watching him in the dark save for a single unflickering candle.

***

When Amnandi awoke, the world was still the world. Bog accepted the gift of breakfast; he and Amnandi spoke of the voyage without embellishments; Khumalo listened appreciatively; Bog eventually took his leave. This was the way of things. Amnandi wasn't happy to see him go, but she was well aware that adults rarely sat still long enough to enjoy the things they wanted.

She, on the other hand, had learned meditation and patience, which served her well, for—after breakfast, meditation, and studies—she was allowed to wander by herself on land, although not entirely alone. She had Natuun with her. Natuun wasn't in a morning listening mood, which, again, served well. It felt like a dawn for silent riding.

Time was often an issue for Amnandi. Not keeping track of it—her internal clock was unrivaled. Living in it, or within one stream of it, felt unnatural. Mother told her everyone had multiple selves, but only a few were ever aware of this fact, and even fewer successfully engaged with it. Amnandi had that gift. Whenever she visited her various selves across the veils, she felt infinite. She'd told her mother this, and Mother had taught her to hold moments as gently but surely as she would a butterfly between thumb and forefinger.

This morning's ride, then, was a butterfly ride.

There was a lot for a ten-year-old to like about this land. It was a lot cloudier than anywhere she and Mother had traveled in Afrela, and she very much enjoyed that gentle feeling of fat, omnipresent lakes traveling above her. The forests there told fanciful jokes rather than learned fables. The mountains lining the distances weren't as tall as the spirit thrones back home, but their jagged, happy smiles were just as inviting. Amnandi and her mother had visited those home mountains, the ones that kept the B'wah Desert bordered on three sides by a crown of clouds that never seemed to deliver their promised plentiful rainfall. Amnandi loved it. The seclusion gave her the sense of her and her mother finally at rest, a permanent, good rest after marvelous travels, because Mother always said the only reason for travel was to create the best possibility for home.

Mother Khumalo defined *home* as *who* you were, not necessarily where. Amnandi had felt a special kind of peace and mental quietude, wandering those craggy mountains, wishing she were like the hooved beasts who clung to upward rock, or the scraggly shrubs that dropped berries whether they ought to or not. They all seemed to know who they were and where they fit best.

Amnandi didn't think they'd make it to the mountains here;

Mother had thus far stayed to the interior and coastal regions. But Bog had. Aboard ship, during a period of dead wind which the captain took as a message of rest for both sails and rowers, the two shared vegetables and strips of dried meat while Bog told stories of facing a wizard in the mountains who'd attempted to foment a war between the wizard's walled people and the forest gods wanting nothing but sleep. It rained every day, he'd said, "The type of rain that urges caution to prevent inevitable tears."

"And the wizard, did he heed?"

"He did not." Bog said this dryly.

Her horse, Natuun, having nibbled at enough scrub during this reverie, raised its head to take an interest in the mountains with her. She patted its neck, sensing its trepidation at undertaking such a journey so early.

"It's too far a ride," Amnandi assured Natuun, "for the morning, at any rate." What good was a magnificent steed if one couldn't tease it from time to time?

The range was a good five days' ride away, if not more, that, of course, at a leisurely pace. "Someday," said Amnandi. "Maybe when I'm older?" she asked the horse.

Natuun was noncommittal.

One other thing she liked about this particular village was its children weren't overly silly. Two other villages she and Mother visited had branded them witches in a bad way. She still didn't forgive the blond-haired girl and her little brother for suggesting Mother had lured them into a large oven to eat them, when both children knew full well that Amnandi had invited them into the oven during play to show them other worlds through the veils. All homes had such portals, usually multiple. Amnandi was good at finding them.

The boy had cried so much at suddenly being somewhere else that the sister panicked. Mother had to reach through and pull them out.

Magick didn't seem quite as threatening at this new place, although Amnandi had learned her lesson to proceed with caution. So far, she'd limited herself to certain tricks with light, which the children she'd become comfortable with found delightful.

She was eager to tell them about her trip.

When she saw them playing at the appointed clearing, she released the reins to give a loud triple whistle. Children there loved noise. She did it again just to be exuberant. It looked like they'd started their weird game of Death and the Farmer: one child—Death—buried clues to a riddle solvable only if all the other children worked together to gather them. The riddles never totally made sense to Amnandi, who wasn't a farming child, but she was fascinated by the process and results nonetheless. The children had to cobble the clues while Death chased them.

She had three friends, which meant only two evading Death. The game immediately paused at Amnandi's signal. Three girls ran toward her.

The eldest, Gita, a year older than Amnandi, yelled, "Travel Girl!"

Amnandi slid her legs over Natuun's back as the horse slowed, and carried the motion into a dismount from the moving pony. She and Gita put their foreheads together in the way of Gita's people, who had journeyed from their home nearly as far as Amnandi's small family. The clouds had not sapped the burnish from her skin. The other two girls were of this land and waited their turn for hugs.

Bettany—the same age as Amnandi—was frost pale with the wispiest eyebrows and lashes Amnandi had ever seen. Upon their first meeting, Bettany had smiled so widely, Amnandi thought they must have been related.

Amis, nine, the youngest solely by a year, always had a smudge somewhere on her freckled face. As well as on her clothing. Since shoes rarely stayed on her for long, her feet too.

Gita asked, "Did you have fun?"

Bettany asked, "Did you bring us treats?"

Amis asked, "Did you kill anything?"

Amnandi laughed, quickly turned to pat Natuun's neck in a way that communicated *Don't wander too far or too long*, then dove back to her friends' glee, motioning for them to step back a bit so she could reach into her invisible pocket of precious things and pull out—in rapid, efficient succession, as magick wasn't meant to be dolorous—a small orb made of blown glass and streaked throughout with all the colors of a sunset, a puzzle of sticks meant to form intricate shapes in as few pieces as possible, and a cloth pouch containing a bright blue feather, the shell of a red snail, and a triangular tooth as long as a babe's pinky finger, serrated as a saw.

"I love when you do that!" said Amis.

Amnandi set each item on the ground, then knelt before them. The three girls knelt as well. They picked unerringly.

Amnandi pointed to the feather in Amis's hand. "The bird fell into the sea like an arrow. It stayed under so long, I thought it had died, so I went to the other end of the ship out of respect. It came out with a fish and left this feather in the water. The captain let a netter fish it out for me. She said lost feathers are blessed by all gods. She has a sarong with at least a hundred different feathers sewn to it. So," Amnandi said, beaming into Amis's face, "you'll be lucky! She says the feathers are stories and a story is not complete until you're able to tell it to someone else."

"I want to be the captain. A hundred feathers? Lucky forever!"

Amnandi made the gesture of heart-to-mind agreement before addressing the orb of glass being turned over in Gita's hands:

"My mother told me that if she ever goes to the stars, she'll ignite a section of night so I can see. That's something you'd do."

Gita's smile was so bright, plants might have done well to lean toward her. "It's like I'm holding heaven."

"Holding heaven," Amnandi said then repeated it two more times so it would stick. Collecting beautiful notions felt good to her brain.

The last, the simple puzzle of sticks, required no explanation, as Bettany had already laid them out with her omnipresent expression of concentration, telling the group she'd have it figured out before sunfall.

"Do you like it?" Amnandi asked. Bettany had a rodent-like appearance to her, which always heightened the look of concentration.

"I do."

"It's hard."

"You're a good friend," Bettany agreed. "Were there wizards?"

"Not that I saw."

"Giants?" asked Amis.

"Only my friend Bog. A small giant. A human giant."

"I've seen him," Bettany countered. "He's as tall as your mother."

"He feels bigger," said Amnandi.

"Favorite part of the voyage?" tossed Gita into the flurry of questions.

"Working on the ship. I think I'll be a sailor at some point."

"A sea witch!" Amis shouted.

"All witches are sea witches. Water is the world," said Amnandi.

There was learned nodding and consensus to this.

"Should we make a pact to explore the world when we're older?" said Bettany.

"We do that now!" said Amis.

"I mean the *world*," Bettany clarified. "My father's experimenting with the exploding powders from the East." She lowered her voice. "It's illegal."

"From Shau?" asked Amnandi.

"Yes! I'd love to go there," said Bettany.

"My mother and I plan to keep going until we're in Afrela again," said Amnandi. "Mother says we're using the entire planet as a portal."

"Your portals are strange," said Bettany.

"Everything wonderful is strange here," said Amnandi. "Too many in these lands remain perpetually frightened."

"What does *perpetually* mean?" said Amis.

"Always and ongoing by choice," said Amnandi.

"We have monsters," said Bettany, eyes going back and forth between sticks in both hands.

"I doubt it. You have *stories* of monsters," said Amnandi, "but no lack of monstrous people. Have you ever seen your tree people or water travelers? Or the small ones? They all know of monsters."

"'They all know of monsters,'" Gita, as elder, mimicked. "Hush, old woman."

"There are monsters in the mountains," said Amis. "Big ones. They eat children."

"You know this?" said Amnandi.

"I've heard old people say," said Amis.

"It was said my mother ate children." Amnandi's voice was suddenly a warning.

"Utterly stupid," said Bettany, still mentally configuring. "But the mountains, well, there are possibilities."

Amis nodded. "Red Lizard, No-Name, and the Splinter live at the tips," she said, studying her feather, the words carrying so little conviction, she forgot them the moment they left her lips.

"But is there proof?" said Amnandi.

The speed of responses slowed considerably.

Amnandi, staring intently at the faces of her three friends, gauged the truth they might be carrying. "Is there *proof*?"

"Castings and bones," said Bettany.

"Talk of them," Gita clarified. "Fairy tales," she said to put the matter to rest.

"Gah, talk! All you do is talk here. Has *no one* tried to speak with their mysteries?"

"Is that from your mother?" said Gita.

"That is me. Mother and I had a home burned because of talk. Anyone speaking to me had better carry truth upon their back."

"Did Bog kill anyone?" This, of course, Amis.

Amnandi threw her hands up. "Why are you so obsessed with death?"

Amis shrugged. "I bet he likes killing people."

"No one likes killing people," said Amnandi.

"Some do," Amis rebutted.

"They aren't people. They're cullers, spirits who attempt to steal more life than balance provides for."

"Your mother teaches you odd things," said Amis.

"Unina teaches me what the world is made of...and how to shape it."

Bettany looked up from her sticks. "We have weird friends."

"We do," said Gita. She raised the swirled rainbow orb high. "Here's to that!"

Amis added her feather to the tribute. "To the one day we don't have chores!" It had been silently agreed upon many times over that this was their favorite spot, Death and the Farmer their favorite game, and these their favorite people, newcomer Amnandi included.

In Amnandi's eyes these were true friends, for none of them

had asked her to teach them magick. They liked how they were; they liked how she was.

"Ships stink," Amnandi confided. "Lots of chores onboard."

"Stinky chores," said Bettany.

"All chores stink," said Amis.

Gita, Bettany, and Amis all looked toward Amnandi expectantly.

"Yes?" said Amnandi.

"We're waiting for you to say you enjoy yours," said Gita. "Because you're weird."

"I don't have to carry cattle," Amnandi answered, looking at Bettany's strong arms, "or juggle poultry"—this at Amis—"but sometimes I have to help figure things out"—Gita—"and that's fun. I like that. A lot." Amnandi paused to consider. "Sweeping is peaceful. Keeping the home neat gives the unseen ones a chance to rearrange while we're away. Cooking is always a joy—"

"Amnandi?" said Gita.

Amnandi stopped short. "Yes?"

Gita set the orb on the grass. "You're Death. Make your riddle!" All three girls immediately popped up to run a good distance away to permit their friend time to think.

"I didn't bring anything to bury!" Amnandi shouted after them.

"Improvise!" all three shouted back, which clearly meant they knew her too well already and had planned for this eventuality.

Games. She was excellent at chase games. Riddles vexed her. Riddles offered up too many possibilities.

Perhaps, rather than clever, she would be literal.

Amnandi knelt, reached into one of her pocket veils, and retrieved the writing tablet and chalk she had used directly after breakfast for the day's science lesson. It was wiped pristinely clean—as it was after every lesson—and always solidly, comfortably cool to the touch, like stone fresh from the river. She kept an eye on her friends (who had their backs to her) and wrote her message in white chalk on the unevenly shaped slate affixed to a tan yuffa-wood backing.

She set the slate down.

She called their names.

They turned.

She was gone.

They looked left and right. There was no way she could have run out of sight that quickly.

But she was Amnandi Khumalo. Her world spun differently. They trotted back to the spot. Gita grabbed the slate and read:

"If I am Death, where do I live?"

Natuun the horse was a good distance away, sampling grasses.

Insects and birds behaved as insects and birds do.

The trees surrounding the clearing did nothing nor hid anything.

It was as though—excepting Natuun's presence—the wild dark child had never been there.

Amis was the first to protest. "Using magick!"

Bettany, turning in a circle to keep all surroundings in view, said, "Well, it's not against the rules..." There was movement by a brackle bush, but it was only a hare. "*We* just can't do it."

"If one can't do it, none should do it," said Amis, fearing a resounding loss.

"That's not how it works," said Bettany. "Gita?"

"We just have to wait her out and look for clues."

"There are no clues. Only this tablet. Which we have," complained Amis.

Amnandi saw and heard them through her mind's eye through the veil of the Green World. She called it that because nearly everything there was green. It was the most lush, verdant space she'd ever had the pleasure of receiving breath from, home to a version of herself who tended to be sad until Amnandi came through. Not woefully sad. Sad, said her other self, for anything that wasn't content.

Her other selves (there were multiple) never left their dimensions for hers, and she certainly wouldn't force it.

"You like them very much, don't you?" Amnandi Green said to Amnandi.

"Yes."

"Will you bring them here?"

"Not likely"

Amnandi the Green gave a heavy sigh and didn't care that Amnandi saw it.

"I told you Mother doesn't want others through the veils unless necessary. Besides which, you are a part of me, so you get to experience them as well."

"As dreams."

"Dreams are the best part of life." Amnandi then shushed her to better concentrate.

"What is the answer to your riddle?" said the Green.

Amnandi put a hand over her own heart.

"Clever," said the Green.

The three girls spread out to search carefully.

Amnandi hugged the Green. "Wish me luck!"

The Green hugged her back. "You'll win."

Amnandi called the portal to her. It seared its heatless, soundless flame through reality and waited, potentiality requiring purpose.

In the dimension containing Waterfall, a quickening wind had driven clouds between the sun and the forest. The morning, very briefly, felt ancient and well used. To Amnandi, it made her friends seem as if they'd aged.

Gita was a teacher wandering the woods.

Amis became an experienced, renowned hunter.

Bettany created new things from the forest's stores.

Amnandi had re-entered the world low to the ground, hidden from view by brackberry bushes. She plucked a handful of brackberries and munched as she watched.

Gita would be first. She was the slowest runner of them all. And once afoot, she was easily confused as to which way to go, as if her left foot and right foot never fully reached consensus.

The clouding made the girls instinctively draw closer together but not exactly close.

Amnandi had never tried portaling so quickly and precisely in front of someone, but she still felt adventurous and, most importantly, was certain she could do it without incident. As far as she knew, even Unina hadn't done it. Or, at least, Amnandi had never *seen* her. But doing so would just be an extension of will and concentration. The hardest would be touching them without her entire body coming through.

Gita, the slowest *and* tallest. A perfect logical trial target.

Amnandi portaled from behind the bushes, popped partially inward in front of Gita, darted her hand forward...and glanced a finger off Gita's left shoulder.

Gita immediately shouted, "That's not funny!" then just as immediately rallied the girls. "Form a circle and watch for heat. I know the answer."

Amis and Bettany rushed to her side, backs to backs.

Amnandi conjured a portal along the branch of a tall tree skirting the clearing and called down, "Where does Death live?" before winking into another hiding place.

Their gifts lay nearby. Gita raced to them, picked hers up, and gave instructions. "Death lives in the heart. Hold your presents in front of your heart."

They snatched each, quickly returning to back-to-back stance.

"We're shielded. You can't touch our hearts. Come out," said Gita. Amnandi popped through a portal in front of her.

"You haven't told *me* the answer to the riddle. Isn't that the rules?" said the witch.

"The Farmers have the answer to your riddle," Gita announced formally. "You can't touch us now. Death lives in *us*."

"This...is a strange game," said Amnandi.

Amis sat cross-legged to hold her feather to the returning sun. "That's a weird riddle," she said, peering one-eyed through the soft gaps.

"We carry our deaths with us at all times. Don't you know that?" said Amnandi.

"I know that I don't want to play this anymore," Amis huffed, "and I want to go to the mountains."

"Why?" asked Amnandi, genuinely curious.

"New things."

Amnandi sat beside her and looked at the sky through the feather, their heads, one wrapped in colorful scarves, the other all wild dirty hair, nearly touching.

Gita and Bettany sat as well. They rolled the aurora-swirled orb between them, then sent it off toward Amnandi and Amis. Eventually, the orb crisscrossed with their conversation, rolling slowly but steadily from girl to girl.

"What if there are dragoons in the mountains?" said Gita. "No one sees dragoons anymore."

"Did they ever, really?" said Bettany.

"Mum says," said Gita.

Amnandi imagined Gita's mother facing a dragoon. "My mother would like your mum."

"Everybody likes my mum. She bakes sweetbreads."

"My da wouldn't let me go into the mountains," said Amis, still considering it an actual possibility.

"It would take us forever," said Bettany.

"If we don't think about our deaths, would we live forever?" said Amis. All eyes went to Amnandi.

Amnandi frowned in confusion at those expectant eyes.

"This is your specialty, Magick Girl," said Bettany.

"I've never died."

"What's your mother said? I'm sure she's given you a lesson on dying." Bettany had heard "*Mother says*" from Amnandi so much, she had actually started writing some of them down.

"She's told me not to. Ever."

"Da says he expects me to live to be four hundred," said Amis. No one asked about her ma. She had died half Amis's lifetime before.

The colorful orb made its way to Amnandi. She let it roll up the ramp of her palm and held it to the returned sun with a dolorous smile at unpredictable mornings and friends to share in it. "I like this very much," she told the group.

"What happens if we get to the mountains and find monsters?" Bettany—ever-practical Bettany—put to Amis.

"We'd figure something out," Amis proclaimed, and proclamation it was, they all felt it. "How could we not?"

***

"Mum, nothing is as we expect it," Amnandi said when she got home, then promptly settled into her corner of the room to read on a woven mat depicting an image of the goddess eating from her favorite tree, a gift from her grandmother upon her fifth birthday.

"*Mum*?" said Mother Khumalo, brow arched.

Amnandi, already a paragraph into her text, did not respond.

"Did you enjoy the sun?" Khumalo said louder.

"I did."

"And you thanked Natuun?"

"I did."

"And hugged your mother?"

Amnandi's head poked up.

"You may save it for later. I," said Mother Khumalo, wrapping her scarves tighter around her head against the outdoor's intention to gust, "shall have my own play for a bit."

"Will you be gone long?"

"No."

"Travel well."

"I will. And I will tell Bog hello for you." Mother grinned Amnandi's way again and exited, silently entreating the house as she closed its door to graciously maintain its protection spell over her child. The presences within the home agreed.

Her horse, the majestic mare Beedma, as reddish brown as dried blood and just as potent, trotted to her, lowered for her, waited till the weight properly settled upon the thick mat Khumalo used as a saddle, then—in the shared privacy of an early morning as they were wont to do—took off at a run so fast, both Beedma and Khumalo gave thanks to the wind for not cutting them.

Since Khumalo—Ayanda to her friends—liked to shelter a fair distance from town proper, they had time for a good sprint: past water, into forest, through a clearing ideal for play, more forest, Beedma's footing sure and steady, Ayanda's eyes and touch sharp and guiding. Beedma would slow when Beedma was ready. The rhythmic *clop*s of her hoofs were the kata drums of home played by a virtuoso faster and faster, the way katans did during the Giving festival, trying their best to tire dancers into giddy heaps.

Beedma had no interest in heaps. She ran until thirsty, drank side by side with Mother Khumalo from a freshwater stream, trotted when underway again, then, when within hearing distance of the seaport village, proceeded respectably, neither too fast nor too slow.

But she never *stopped*. Beedma would ride halfway around the world if need be. Not pride. Dedication.

Once within the village proper, Beedma became just another horse, whereas her rider would never be mistaken for just another rider.

Ayanda—Mother—Khumalo stood high even when sitting. Back straight, head and spine a perfect balancing act. And ever the most colorful flag to take flight in the wind. Three scarves, orange, pale green, and sunrise gold, made up the day's headpiece. Her inner robe: lapis blue. Outer: earth brown. Breezy, functional, and exceedingly comfortable, three things no one in this land had yet to consider her.

What, beyond wanderlove and curiosity, had brought them there? This was their fifth month in Eurola, fourth week in the trading port of Waterfall. Three weeks of knowing Bog. A curious person, he was, both literally and in review of his temperament. It wasn't that he was a loner, for it was never difficult finding a small crowd around him; it wasn't that he was in need of constant distractions, for there were times, plenty of them, when Ayanda Khumalo saw him walk off alone. He seemed not to have a destination for those walks, and she left him the courteous privacy such wandering deserved.

He'd been in Waterfall a full month himself at various jobs, but there was no missing the mission in everything about him, from the set of his shoulders to the hawk's searching in his eyes whenever he appeared to be looking at nothing. No missing, that is, to those accustomed to seeing.

Beedma recalled where he lived, so Khumalo was able to focus on the general feel of the village. No matter where she went in the world, there was always unease in its populace. Even the varied peoples she'd visited outside her home city of Insheree held worries. Here, though, worries remained held too closely to the chest; worries became heartbeats and, thus, in a strange way, comforts. But at first arriving in Waterfall? The unease was sharp. A briar underfoot.

And it had everything to do with Twitswaddle. The Thief Mage. There was no predator so low as a scavenger pretending to be a hunter.

Fortunately, she *was* a hunter.

She had not come to this place to hunt.

Mercy could be a complicated blessing to bestow.

A witch will not lie to herself, Khumalo reprimanded. *We will not call hubris mercy. You were as foolish as a child.*

Beedma's muscles shifted ever so slightly whenever they passed a stall selling sweetbreads—Ayanda's favorites—to the morning laborers moving unhurriedly but steadily toward the docks. Sweetbreads and dried meat. Food for standing, cursing, or sweating with a moment or two to chew. There were many such stalls, each open-air box structure of the cheapest wood possible, advertising its wares with the sole extravagance on display from there to the docks—an ornate green tile set into the lintel—but Ayanda wanted none. She patted Beedma's flank in thanks each time, though, until Beedma realized this was a straight-through trip.

Straight through the meal zone, slowly past the scattering of lost ones liable to leap in front of a moving horse or loaded cart without a moment's notice, past Warehouse Row—which, for being four huge, dirty, gray rectangles of clapboard and stone, actually seemed impressive, given the surroundings. They were constantly full of nonperishable goods from every part of the world, constantly guarded, and a constant reminder of what was important to Waterfall. The stables were just beyond the row, and just beyond that the itinerants' lodging.

The lodging always smelled of fish, salt, urine, and a day's hard sweat. It had gained the name "Nowhere," the first question pleasure merchants asked of newcomers to the dock's constant influx and exodus of workers being "Where are you staying?"

"Nowhere."

Nowhere was as drab as the warehouses but nowhere near as majestic. Lacked the size. Lacked any pretense of economic gravitas.

What it did have were outdoor showers with actual lukewarm water, roofed and fenced but without any mind toward privacy. There was usually a throng of pleasure merchants loitering near the stalls regardless of time of day. Few things made a person lustier than getting cleaned up in the hopes of becoming filthy.

Ayanda swung her legs over Beedma's spine and slid down her horse's side. After tying her off—for form's sake—the tall, berobed woman took three steps before she heard the expected—

"Madam Khumalo."

—from an old man who gave the best massages within several days' ride—and on a seaport where muscles were guaranteed to end the days as knotted as ships' rigging, if not more, from any number of hells, not a soul within those showers ever turned him away.

He had taken to calling her Madam Khumalo since first introducing himself days after she'd arrived in Waterfall, knowing someone keeping themselves as constrained as she could use a massage.

She'd politely declined the massage without telling him her name in kind, he abruptly trailed after her, she asked why he was following, he said he felt he needed to know her—all utterly respectful. She responded, truthfully, that her plan was to get to know no more than five people within the village. He'd acknowledged that with a bow and turned to leave.

"Khumalo," she said before he left. "Tell no one my name."

He acquiesced and returned to business.

And had been the most excellent source of clandestine information since.

Today, at the sound of his voice, she turned to him with warmth in her eyes. Because he was a poor man, invisible everywhere he went, he always seemed to appear out of nowhere. "Stepple," said Mother Khumalo, "you're doing well."

"The advice you gave worked miracles on my night terrors," he said. He'd had many reasons to suspect getting to know this woman was a beneficial idea. One of the reasons he had followed her that first time was that he had been to war and sensed she knew the cure for it. (When he had finally asked her, she had answered, "Peace," and then elaborated on two succinct meditation techniques.)

"May we speak when you're done?" he now asked. This meant he had gifts for her.

"Of course," she said, smiling down at him.

Bog always showered in the stall closest to Nowhere's rear entrance. The fencing hid most people—not counting the easy view between half-hearted slats which bothered neither users nor audience—but Bog stood taller than most. Whereas only the heads of every gender blessing the world showed over the fence like a line of wet apples bobbing along the line, his upper torso remained visible from shoulders to mid-chest.

In at least a nod to propriety, onlookers didn't stand right at the fence, nor were they so far away they couldn't carry a conversation should circumstances dictate.

Bog tugged a release chain to clear soapy water from his face. He noted Khumalo's approach. "I was a bit later rising than I expected," he called out. He took a large iron key from a peg and tossed it over the fence to her.

"You were already clean," she said.

"But not fully awake. And I like the smell of this soap. I'll be up shortly."

His room contained what might charitably be called a bed by someone planning to abscond with a charity's takings. There was an actual working toilet, the newer kind upgraded from merely being indoor outhouses. The Nowhere's proprietor figured if it gave tenants working toilets, indoor showers approached outrageous greed.

A stout, hinged crate for personals was nailed to the floor between the bed and the inward-swinging door, clearing space on either side by a finger.

Mother Khumalo sat atop this and waited. She didn't pretend to know Bog any more than this bare room did. Yet she knew that if he thirsted, she would provide water for him. When he hungered, there was food. She knew she could trust the same of him of her. Those who saw the demons that others overlooked mattered to each another.

She knew he traveled, perhaps as far-ranging as herself. She knew they shared the same homeland. She knew from introductory vetting conversations that he'd traveled from Nasthra, but she didn't know where he was born. She knew he harmed no one who did not demand to be harmed, and protected those too trusting to ask for protection.

She knew he would have shattered that ship before seeing her daughter, Amnandi, mistreated in any way.

A beetle attempted to invade his room. She bade it leave. The room may have been relatively barren, but it was clean. Boots in a corner, shin guards beside them. The trunk she sat on exuded no odors. There were no bones on the floor, no crumbs for mice or small folk, and certainly nothing a dart beetle needed to root through.

Leave the man his peace.

When she felt the vibrations of his footfalls upon the second-floor stairs, she stepped out of the room to give him privacy. He passed her without a word, his coarse robe plastered to him, burlap to a rain-laden tree.

The door closed. She waited. The door opened. She entered. He had yet to don his brown tunic, but the gray, tough breeches were in place, as well as his socks, feet getting stuffed into their boots. He perched at the edge of the bed. She resumed her station on the trunk, leaving the door open, as was his habit when he was in the room.

"The water folk wouldn't be happy at your excess," she said.

He glanced up from tying off a boot. "The water folk haven't come off two weeks' voyage where they did everything but tug the boat by a toothsome rope. Sailing is extremely hard work."

"I thought you slept well."

"Well enough. Needed more water."

"For clarity," nodded Khumalo.

Bog nodded as well, took up his shin guards, and affixed them.

"I'm afraid I may have been foolish when you were gone," Khumalo admitted.

"I'd hope so."

"I put a stop to a thief's ways but not to the thief himself."

"Which of that is foolish to you?" On with the tunic, his eyes questioning hers the entire time.

"I'd merely like you to be vigilant."

The eyes narrowed considerably at her.

"*More* vigilant."

He brushed wrinkles from the chest of the tunic. "I aspire to paranoia. I can do that."

She softened a bit, knowing he'd gotten the subtle message to be watchful. "This thief is no longer a danger to anyone but may prove an annoyance based on...information...I've received."

"Understood."

"You will know him less by his description and more by his acts, should action become necessary."

"Let's hope it doesn't become necessary."

Fully dressed, he looked nothing more than a simple peasant, albeit a towering rock of one. She noted he had no weapons on him.

"What are you doing today?" he asked.

She'd been about to ask him the same.

"This is a morning for wandering," she said. "Would you care to wander with me?"

"Where's the small Khumalo?"

"Amnandi's done her wandering."

"I don't generally wander *with* people."

Khumalo stood. "Then you shall enjoy my company all the more for the novelty. I have one stop to make first."

"Regarding your annoyance?"

"Likely."

Stepple, never far from his usual spot, hobbled from the low railing he sat on and made his way to her on sight as rapidly as his aching back allowed, doing an excellent job of pretending to give no particular notice of the person beside her, mountain to her sky-reaching tree. The man—Bog—and Madam both felt ancient, rooted in ways Stepple imagined he would never come to know.

Stepple did, however, know there was no need asking if they could speak; if someone had leave to stand by Madam Khumalo, that person was meant to hear.

As someone who'd been to war and was forever changed by it, he spoke succinctly. "There's intent on the wind, mentions of a brother and a sister."

"Thieves as well?"

Stepple nodded.

"Traveling from?"

"A ways off. The thief says a week, perhaps two."

"How do you come by this?" rumbled the mountain in a tone that said anything less than good information would be unfortunate.

Anyone standing beside Madam Khumalo was deserving of an answer, in Stepple's estimation. "Massaged the horse of a boy who took dried meat to him. Boy spoke of messenger birds and mumbling."

"Get the location from the boy," said Khumalo. "The thief likely has several hideaways."

"Will do my best, ma'am."

Khumalo smiled warmly at him. He felt another of his aches go completely away. Even his back, tired from all the standing and stooping, stood him immediately straighter.

"Be well, friend," said Khumalo.

Stepple waved her toward her day, saying, "Getting better all the time...until I mess meself up again." He parted with a good nod to Bog, who returned it in kind.

When Stepple was out of earshot, Bog leaned to Khumalo's ear and said, "Witchcraft is having good informants."

"Perhaps ninety percent."

***

Bog moved gently. She liked that. It spoke of knowledge of himself in the world, which, in Khumalo's experience, was always of benefit. The small blue flowers along the forest trail's edge were crushed only as couldn't be avoided by someone with a large gait and huge feet.

"Did you know your daughter refused to learn to curse on the ship?"

Khumalo laughed, and she was additionally pleased to know he didn't find gaiety from her surprising. A reputation for being stern seemed to precede her in Eurola, whether a town, village, or hamlet had heard tales of her or not.

"She said," Bog continued, "space for thought was limited, that she didn't want to waste it."

"That," admitted Khumalo, "she got from me." She would be sure to cook Amnandi a special treat for dinner.

"That was my studied suspicion." Bog held his face to the sun as he walked. A wind gust churned all the scents of bluestars, green grass, and the scaly tang of a nearby stream into a sharp, memorable perfume replete with anonymous life.

Khumalo wondered if he experienced it as such. People experienced most—if not all—of life separately and differently. A clear blue sky could be calming or a thing of terrifying, crushing loneliness.

Yet she noted the brief, deeper inhalation he took.

It was a pleasant walk. Bees did bee things, trees spoke of Khumalo and Bog with approval, the wind, as it moved branches and the tips of bushes to change the shadows, invited contemplations of art, impermanence, and flexibility. Their footfalls fell muted upon the most wonderful mixture of grasses, soil, and dry, dusty earth.

"She took to sailing quite well," he said.

"She's meant to travel."

He took a deeper, more obvious breath of pleasure. "We all are."

"And your travels?"

"Not as enjoyable as I'd like. Yours?"

"Very much so."

Bog grunted. Khumalo waited to hear what he'd add to this pronouncement.

"Tales of your travels are taking root," he said. "Have you decided to pluck them or let them flower?"

"It's likely best if I'm vigilant in curating," she said. "There've been instances where tales have endangered my daughter." She paused to hold his full attention. "I will not tolerate that."

"We're agreed. Amnandi has a friend in me."

"She's told me. Making friends is not particularly easy for her. We don't let an abundance of people into our lives. She considers you family and wants to regard you with an honorific."

"I told her not to. I'm only Bog. It's all I need be."

"I'd like you to reconsider. Respect is not at surplus in this land. Perhaps this can be a root from her that spreads. Even the beggar woman found you acceptable."

He frowned. "Beggar woman?"

"You may not have noticed her. She, however, took your measure."

Another grunt, more thoughtful in tone. "What honorific?"

"One from home. 'Balagon.'"

"A two-pronged word. The Wufanyi people. It means protector and teacher. I'm neither."

"But you're good. The good do those things whether they attempt them or not."

"Is this important to you, Khumalo of the Coastal Lands?"

"Ayanda of wherever I please"—her tone playful enough to let him know it was indeed important.

He nodded graciously.

She smiled at his decision.

"*Balagon* sounds better than my given name, anyway," he said.

"So true."

They walked in silence a few paces. He sighed again. It made her very sad for him, knowing he was imagining the end of even this small, brief respite. A life divorced of these simple pleasures became flattened into only what was, not what it could be.

"We're very much alike," she told him, with hope. There were times all one needed was a compassionate voice in order to let go of certain things.

"If I ever have a child, I'll name her Amnandi."

"That would not be as confusing to me as you believe."

They'd reached a section she loved most, a trickle of a stream that made more noise over its jumble of rocks than it seemed it should be able, as if this specific part of their world had something needful to say. She slowed her step to allow him extra time to appreciate its gentle loveliness. Grass grew taller and more robust along the stream's banks. Less a stream than a gouge dragged into the earth by a giant's twig. Perhaps that was its message. That giants passed through there.

She glanced at Bog's face and thought the assessment apt.

"Ayanda," he said after a moment, "if there's any real danger, I'm pledged to you. My sword will answer."

"And your axe?"

"The axe," he explained, "falls only in times of perilous doom."

Ayanda stepped around a frog that had no intention giving way. "Let us then hope the end of the world not make its appearance here." She gestured at the woods around them. "The children play near here often. We shall do the necessary duties to avoid their learning anything of doom."

"You've never killed anyone, have you? Is that what made you let him live?" asked Bog.

"Death doesn't require the aid of Ayanda Khumalo. It is efficient enough."

Bog's grunt this time was directed away from her and at the

world he knew.

Neither wished to speak further of death.

"As fools go, you barely rank, Madam Khumalo."

"High praise."

"What should I expect of this thief?"

"Cowardice. A knife in the back. Poisoned fruit."

"The buffet of venal ills."

"Bribed by a sense of importance too unwieldy to be of benefit. Gorged to the point of self-harm."

"We can...relieve him of that particular burden." *We*, quietly, meaning himself.

"I noticed your shin guards are somewhat...weathered."

"Bitten," he corrected. "Bitten many times over. And you, my friend, wear none."

"I prefer to think anything with such intentions would speak to me before action was taken. Accords may be made."

"I'd wager there's not a snake alive that'd want your displeasure."

"You'd be indeed surprised."

"Why haven't I seen you in these woods before?" he asked.

"You have. You turned away when you did so." She laid a hand on his shoulder. "I respect your privacy. I require your honesty."

The set of his jaw aligned at that. Apology made. Promise given.

"Have you always been so—" he said.

"Annoying?" she said, her voice a grin. Two doves, foraging, took off at their approach. She and Bog paused to watch their ascent.

Resuming their walk, Bog answered Khumalo with his own grin. "Aware."

"On my fifth birthday, I convinced a boar not to attack my father. Finding an accord with it seemed the thing to do. That's the only awareness I possess: that I am able to change the course of things I should be able to change."

"The course of this stream, are you powerful enough to change it?"

"This stream is perfect and beautiful."

"The course of my thoughts?"

"Are they honorable? Do they carry you through reality or shield you from it?"

"I would hope unshielded from you."

"Sit, friend. Let's listen to the water a bit. Thoughts will be unnecessary."

They sat, the water's rhythms eventually lulling them into as peaceful a space as either needed at that particular moment. The wind blew the surface toward the opposite shore. The moment the wind died down, the water doubled back and chased it. Both sides of the narrow stream clapped softly with delight.

"Will you come eat with us later?"

"I will, Ayanda Khumalo of wherever you wish."

"It's a good place to be."

Bog the Unsmiling's wonderful smile didn't go unnoticed by her.

They watched for fish hunting insects that skittered the water as though composing hurried poems. They watched reeds part and come back together, depending on the force of the wind. They watched the wide world for a bit and did not feel a need for the world to notice them.

CHILL

There was a saying among those who dealt with demons: first, determine a demon's worth, then bind it to your intent. Bind it in such a way that when it moves, it feels the barbs tearing at its flesh and calls this a caress.

This one had long before eaten the last morsel of her demon. Which is why she had sight beyond sight, and the ability—hidden to all—to hear thoughts should they be potent enough to call her name. *Raggle*.

A skittering mass of bones, she was, with nails like ice picks or teeth like claws, depending on her meal. With eyes that hated being awake, and a visage that hated what it saw.

She wished to be alone.

And yet...not only had the bird come, but Twitswaddle's message—sent but not sent, like a vapor of fear made into the perfect javelin—her name *needed* in his affairs, her presence *demanded* by his pained soul, roused her from the center of her massive rock where she fed on the ichor of sad, forlorn dreams from deep within the mountains, from the dragoons themselves, whom she lied to in their dream state that the world would never be for them again. In this way, she did not have to feed on the dreams of animals—or humans—again.

In this way, she was left alone.

The world, for its sake and if asked, did not miss a single dubious benefit of her presence.

Raggle had the mind of a very old dragoon skewered and was enjoying its writhing immensely, its confusion not knowing who dared trespass, its fear knowing it could not shake her away, the cold dread of it knowing someone would drain its glories away, leaving it a comatose husk within a chrysalis of volcanic glass.

Twitswaddle tugged weakly on the line between them.

Raggle.

Gods be cast again! But he was family. She and her two brothers had formed this bond through their need to feed. In a sense to feed off each other. Twitswaddle, the Spirit Drinker. Bash, the Bone Grinder.

Raggle of the Ill Bed.

None of them as aware of anything in the world as they ought to have been but fervent in the knowledge that a desire had was a desire to be sated.

She had sent her message that she would come, and yet still she felt her name. Was he so fevered, she was to hear this delirium all her days?

She had heard nothing from her other brother, Bash, for years. Heard nothing from him now. He ate his bones in silence, scraped his marrow in secret. Fitting and right. None needed to see or hear.

She would have her silence again.

Fitting and right.

But she must only come at night. It wouldn't do for the tangle of *things* she was made from to be seen under her brother's sun, not unless necessary.

For now, the day wind howled outside her mountain home, enough to keep the fauna fearful and the multitude of scurriers in their dens, and that—despite the interruption by her adoptive brother—kept her happy.

***

Amis Emty Dotrig combed her hair legitimately every morning, despite later appearances. She conscientiously washed her hands whenever opportune.

And she was incessantly in love with possibility.

Currently she was seventeen apples tall, provided they weren't the very big ones but the smallish deep pinks that fit perfectly in both her dirty palms and grew wild throughout the forest. She knew this because Bettany (whom Amis had tried to trade a chicken for the puzzle of sticks Amnandi had given her simply because that was what friends did) had done the math. Amis considered herself more seventeen plus a half-eaten one, but precision was best left to scientists, witches, and teachers.

Da always said "currently" changed fast. Her, for example. He swore when she told him Bettany's measurement she had been twelve apples but a week before. By late-season harvest, she'd be an entire bushel, he guffawed.

Da always laughed at his jokes. She liked that about him.

What she didn't like was when he was angry with her, like now because she hadn't tended the coops like she was supposed to and like she'd said she would after he reminded her twice.

Fowl seemed intentionally messy. They watched as she cleaned feathers and twigs from the interior of the coop, each puffy avian body ready with precision droppings. Since they didn't have mouths, it was difficult for them to appear amused...but not impossible.

When done with the interior, she poured a bucket of rainwater over the ramp leading into the coop. It had been a good day up to now. Time with friends. Time alone with her new feather with Da repairing holes on the roof of the house. Plenty of time to fall into a deep, dreamy sleep...until Da woke her by tossing a chicken onto her bed.

"Will you be happy when you've rested us to starvation?" he'd said, then immediately shooed her and the chicken outdoors.

Cleaning a coop at dusk, as she did now, was its own special pain. The ground fowl kept wanting to enter, and crowded her legs. Now and then, one slipped past.

"I haven't changed the hay yet!" Amis shouted. Really at all birds in general. They had lucky feathers, which was nice, but all they did was poo everywhere and demand food.

Dusk whisked away the features of the mountain range, but she knew them by heart. Crags, juttings, and gaps. Another child losing its teeth. Big for its age.

Ma had said the range was Amis's sister. That if her small, wild daughter ever went there, she was to protect it. Treat it with the respect it was due. At least that's what Da told her. Amis had to think hard to remember Ma.

But the mountains? Imprinted forever.

BONE

All three ersatz siblings had been chased into the mountain range. It had been so long before that even the people living at the range's shadow spoke of it as vague stories. Fictions. Twitswaddle, Bash, and Raggle were things meant for amusement, their real names no longer used. In stories, Bash was Red Basilisk. Twitswaddle was the Sliver. And Raggle...in stories, Raggle had no name. She was a nightmare taught to walk.

Bash dragged the carcass of a huge buck over rocks and scrub, pausing to stare upward at the spectacle of waning light. Pausing to snap a piece of the equally huge, tree-limb tines from the buck's antlers and munch in his solitude. Birds didn't like to deliver messages to him. He'd eaten the bones of too many feathered messengers, leaving a pall above his head they sensed well. It had forced Twitswaddle to make a rare personal visit to him long past, demanding Bash cease. Important messages were meant to go back and forth, not die at Bash's doorstep.

Not that he had a door. He had a cave. And in this cave he had three boulders to beat bodies against to vary his stores of bones: big bones, medium bones, snack bones.

He ground the buck's antler between gray molars big as thumbs, enjoying the mossy, hairy tang it released. This carcass would be perfect for snack bones. Only three or four whacks.

He didn't even remember how they—people, of all things—had managed to chase *him* (or Raggle, or Twit, but mostly *him*) into the mountains. The importance of remembering such had faded a long time before. The only reason he remembered not always having lived in the mountains was that he missed big fish. Large sea things he often dragged from a silty bottom to crack against the hulls of ships if boulders couldn't be found. Fish with sharp teeth and angry dead eyes were best. Many rows of teeth. Much cracking between his own. There were no such fish in these mountains.

The latest message had been *Help me*, and had been signed with the bird dying in a flap of large wings and sudden weakness. This was not a message that needed response. It was a summoning. Although, yes, there was a message specifically for Bash in its dying. Death meant he could eat the bones. When he'd swallowed, his brother spoke through their marrow: directions, commands, images. The image was of an obsidian knife in human form. The image spoke of revenge needed, of humiliation endured, and of a poison to his soul that drained him daily.

Her bones are your bones, said the dead bird's marrow, coiling around the image. *Avenge your brother. Take her bones. Take the bones and chew.*

Each step Bash took away from his home and toward the distant dark, toward where his brother had managed to return, a memory of never being hungry was added.

***

For seven generations, the village of Waterfall had grown at the flat end of the Great Crescent range. Slowly and surely as a barnacle, it crusted over plots of land that had once been covered in leaves, or had run wild with fowl, or—in the case of the sea— teemed with so much unspoiled life that not even the merfolk had need to sample the errant human or two.

Its great harbor was situated within decent sailing distance of archipelagos, islands, even its own coastal peoples. The waters, being calmed by the Great Range's crescent reaching its sloping fingers into the sea, were deemed ideal for ships by those who knew the needs of wooden whales.

And the fact that, from the coast to the craggy feet of the mountains, so many different trees became the brightest paint during the cooler months, so many that settlers and visitors alike had stopped trying to name them, placed a capstone and transformed the land, sea, and sky in that part of Eurola into what it had never considered itself before: a place. A place even of importance. Certainly of value to its inhabitants.

Waterfall.

Full of tumbling, drifting, splashing people.

Travelers came in, but those who lived there, its weary inhabitants, remained in the surf and foam, wandering from one need to another.

But not always having that need fulfilled.

Orsys the beggar woman had been born there, made her life there, succeeded at life until she didn't, and continued to wander there.

Stepple, during several periods of Waterfall's prosperity, had been in wars to preserve that wealth, yet was not meant to partake of that wealth. The guilds partook of wealth. Such was the way of things, and such was how Waterfall grew.

It grew and grew.

And at some point matured.

Or, at the very least, convinced its citizenry it had.

The ships built there were not only the largest but the fastest.

The goods traded there were not only the newest of familiar items but new items destined to become useful heirlooms. Items sent by wizards, thinkers, and artisans.

The warehouses, massive things that put visitors in mind of holy places, cemented Waterfall's importance. Neighborhoods and enclaves sprung up around each warehouse's mass, tiny villages within villages.

There had been peace now for five whole years. A run like that spread its reputation and brought travelers, workers, and the more-than-occasional thief.

Ayanda Khumalo, in journeying Eurola's varying climes, sensed that peace and directed herself and her daughter to it, particularly after having been recently chased from one settlement, having had to do battle with grieving spirits in another, and then wandering away from—not toward—people for a brief recuperative time after that.

The famed port city, and city it was despite it wanting to lay claim to "village," had seemed a place of anonymous scrabbling activity. Human crabs not knowing the soul or destination of the beast they rode but knowing they must keep it clean.

Ayanda had ridden into the village from the gate road, Beedma *clip-clop*ping slowly like a bored drummer, rode through the garment district, the general goods district, the foods of many tastes district, all the way past the warehouses, past the docks, and straight to the farthest wharf, where she dismounted, tied off Beedma, and walked to the outermost tip of the wharf jutting over the sea. She then spoke to the calm waters in the highly unexpected solitude of midday in a bustling port.

She asked the water if it had created this private spot so that they may speak undisturbed.

The water barely answered, save for soft laps against wood.

Khumalo took that to be enough.

Amnandi, beside her, still atop smaller Natuun, gave her mother the nod of agreement.

Waterfall. A place that had no waterfalls. A place, according to snatches of conversation lodged in the air, given to weather extremes: too hot in the summer, too wet in the spring, annoyingly blustery during fall—the most beautiful fall, frequently said and fiercely maintained, in the entire known world-- with its winters being stories of dread.

The one agreeable constant: the sea.

In summer: calm.

In spring: inviting.

In fall: an old friend.

Winter: a grandmother, slow in her gait, exact in her movements, full of future dreams while at rest.

Bitterly cold when affronted.

Khumalo had no plans to be anywhere near this continent's frozen coast during winter, but a stay through perhaps mid-autumn would do. Lodging would be no problem, as there were always cottages scattered in the forests, or huts just on the outskirts of any community. Often those who lived alone were eventually found by family dead alone, with their shoddy houses subsequently left to ruin.

A shoddy home was but a joy's cleaning and repairing to a witch.

She rode out of Waterfall entirely unaccosted, her daughter beside her.

Through autumn would do.

"And so the first time I saw your mother," said Bog, "she was carrying a rain barrel above her head. It remains one of the most delightful things I've ever seen. The strength of three."

"Four at least," said Khumalo.

"Four and their families," said Bog.

"It was an old, ragged barrel," said Khumalo. "The shopkeeper said I could have it if I removed it from his doorway along with the dirty water within it." Khumalo caught Amnandi's rapt gaze. "Not a drop spilt."

"And that is how you came to have such a marvelous tub," said Bog.

"Half of it," said Amnandi.

"Oh? You know the other half of this tale? Speak, scribe!" said Bog.

"The other barrel was found atop a boulder in the woods—"

"No explanation for its presence," said Mother.

"None," said Amnandi. "But sturdy enough for the two to fuse."

"And this," said Bog, "is how small things become important things." Then he patted his belly. "And *this* is how big things become even bigger. If I eat here any more often, I'll have to leave wages to the house."

"At the very least, I will never charge you for hot water," said Khumalo.

"Will you tell me how you heat water with no flame? If I'm to become invulnerable by bathing in a magic tub, I'd like to be able to speak on the how of it," said Bog.

"Let us say water is easily excitable," said Khumalo. "Particularly when told people of good spirit need its blessings."

Bog would not defer his spirit in front of Amnandi. Instead, he asked the young one, "And you, on land as of now eight days, are your bones pining for water again?"

"Not as yet, Balagon, but they will."

He tutted her. "At your table, in your home, I am your friend. Outside..."

"Outside, they need to know in whose presence they walk," said Amnandi.

"Agreed," Bog said.

"Agreed," said Amnandi.

Ayanda's smile was all the agreement needed from her edge of the round rug.

There were still at least three hours of summer daylight before the universe settled upon them. Amnandi picked up their three bowls, balancing them easily in the crook of an arm, then rolled up the mat upon which had sat bread, raw vegetables, and two oily, spicy dips inside hollowed orange rind halves, all gone now. She kissed her mother's unwrapped forehead, touched her own scarved forehead to Bog's, settled the clay dishes in a wash basket, and made for the door.

"Have them home by dark," said her mother.

"And myself here a moment after that," Amnandi said. "*Dazeet*, Unina." She frowned a moment. Fun awaited *her*, but for these old people? "What will you do while I'm away?"

"We will," Unina Khumalo announced, "amuse ourselves."

***

Ayanda nearly laughed when she spun away from the blow Bog thought he had timed so perfectly as to finally gain the advantage in points. Where she kept padded training staffs in the small shack, he didn't know. He had learned it didn't matter to question. Ayanda Khumalo was a witch. Witches accomplished witchy things.

But he suspected she had not used witchery to evade his blow. The impromptu spar had been at her suggestion. She was clearly no stranger to martial practices.

They circled one another in the grass behind the shack.

Her footing was sure, though her left foot gave away her intentions more often than she realized. He suspected she was not aware she favored pushing off from it for upper-body attacks.

Her strikes, however, were flawless. Her evasions, often unique in their geometries. A twist coupled with a sudden spin here. A total reversal of motion more like time turning itself backward than a human body reacting. She was quick and she was accurate. Her eyes missed nothing except her own left foot.

Its heel left the ground, slightly and quickly, a decision being made.

She was going to try for another reversing spin.

The left foot pushed off. Khumalo rotated clockwise, the staff held close to her lithe body. Almost immediately, her right hip arched to receive the momentum from the right foot, which slapped down and pushed her into counterrotation quick as a rapier spun like a top, the staff—in a blink—above her head for a downward strike to Bog's forward ankle.

She missed. Too easily. She noted this.

His staff swung down and up, clacking hers hard enough to send her into a new stance. Completing its circle, the staff swept her left foot from under her.

She went down with a hearty laugh, twisting to allow the thick grass to absorb her fall. She continued laughing, making no move to get up. Instead, she folded her arms behind her head for better comfort and stared upward.

Bog settled beside her, resting his staff down his body at his chin as though prepared to play the world's largest flute.

"Will we spend many nights watching the sky, my friend?" he

asked.

"I think yes."

"Until you leave."

"Or you. You've the greater time spent here. That much closer to goodbye," said Khumalo. She sat up a bit and looked at him. "*Bog the Unsmiling* is quite a lie." Then back down again, looking skyward for points of light. The beginning of starlight was not to be missed.

"Who taught you the Western school?" Bog asked.

"My mother. Head of the cavalry. My father was a gardener."

"What was life like back home for you? Not just as a child."

"Insheree is wonderful. Trees dripped energy like sap and you couldn't drink from *any* stream without tasting magick. I miss my childhood. I wandered all over Afrela, but Insheree is home. My adulthood brought my lover, then my daughter. A perfect continuum."

"What of him?"

"Returned to energy before Amnandi had learned to spell his name."

Bog automatically closed his eyes and touched two fingers to the space between them. "His memory provide sight."

"It does."

"Has she seen him as a ghost?"

"No. At his request. 'I don't want her to see me like this.' He felt death diminished him." She sat up again. She did not usually sit up so much. "How do you feel about death?"

"Unavoidable. At times a necessity for the peace of the living."

She lay back. "Has your life ever brought you peace?"

"May I answer that question after some thought?"

"Always my preference." She asked her last weighted question but didn't sit up for it. "Why here? I know what drew you; I felt a similar needful energy. What keeps you?"

"Beyond grass, company, and stars?"

"The stars are not out yet."

"Stars are fascinating. Always there but only seen on their own schedule." He shifted the staff under the scrag of his chin and idly fingered its smoothed wood as if playing a tune. "I sought work. I got involved in a war between three wizards on the way here. One wanted the power of the other, the other wanted the wealth of another, the last had welcomed cruelty as a meal. This was a month of my life before arriving here. Work tends to quell ghosts. I gave the lodging house my coin, they safeguarded my weapons save a few boot knives, I took work at the docks." This time, it was he who sat up. The witch needed his eyes at this next. "There are three less wizards in the world."

"I have wondered when you might confide in me."

He answered only with the sound of deeper breathing.

"Those are powerful ghosts to have in your head," said Ayanda Khumalo.

Now the breathing shallowed. Constraint.

"If you grunt," she said as the first group of stars poked through the tissue of the purple sky, "I will take away your soup privileges."

"You're very cruel, Ayanda Khumalo."

"Shall I withhold peppered flatbread as well?" She rolled to her knees, crawled behind him, lifted his head, and placed it in her lap. "Do nothing besides breathe," she said, her knees at either side of his head like blinders to a horse. She allowed him only one path, and he knew this. "How many do you hold in there?" she asked gently.

He took her to mean all the dead. "Scores."

"I have no covenant with any not touched by magicks."

"Three will do."

"Do nothing but breathe."

And he did, eventually losing the welcoming sensation of her fingertips grazing different parts of his scarred bald head now and then, as if strumming the odd notes of an instrument no one else had yet seen.

At first, he tried following the touches with his mind's eye, trying to grasp the pattern of her ministrations, but the admonition she implanted held sway. *Do nothing but breathe.*

He breathed until he breathed himself down to a fine dot, and then, with one breath more, to nothing.

When he awoke, it was dark. Amnandi tended a stone-ringed fire nearby, the flames highlighting her as a small god of her own making. He raised his head from a lumpy sack pillow that still smelled of barley.

"Your mother?"

"Soaking. She had to use her mask to pull them out. She gets tired when she does that."

A mask was one of the deepest magicks of Afrela, said to impart energies humans were right to view with respect. If she had done that for him... "You...sensed them too?"

She nodded over the flames. She watched his ghosts in the flames, unseen by him, three pale yellow sparks jumping from lick to lick in search of a new universe to infect.

"What type of world must you two live in?" he muttered.

"It is this one," said Amnandi, taking her eyes from the eternal dance to answer him. She gazed at the fire again. Energies bounced amongst the flames as through a hall of mirrors. Unseen by Bog again, Amnandi widened her eyes briefly. The fire brightened accordingly. There was no pain in there, but there was no escape, either. When the flame went out, they would know peace.

Bog rolled to his feet, leaving Amnandi to the warm night.

Khumalo and the oakwood tub were nearly invisible behind the house, but now and again her wet skin or the gently undulating water reflected a glint from the stars, moon, or whatever unseen forces were about.

"Are you well, Ayanda?"

"I am."

He felt the tub's warmth as he moved closer. It was the type of warmth that drew one toward it, even on a summer night. The warmth of being.

"How long have you been in here?" he asked.

"Minutes. Amnandi has barely been home long enough to settle."

"I think she was watching over me."

"She was."

"Thank you."

"It was a recent burden, easily unbound." There was no need to tell him of the cancerous erosion that could have resulted within his mind had they not been removed.

"I remain indebted to you."

"Sit with me," she said.

He sat, able to see an elbow over the side of the tub, able to just make out the profile of her face but not its features.

"This is payment enough," she said.

***

A week later, a strange visitor knocked once, twice, then thrice upon Khumalo's door. This visitor was strange in that she wore finery, had an entourage, and seemed to think that giving Khumalo a certificate was important.

"You *are* Madam Khumalo?" said the visitor, a woman so pale, she could be considered a light source. Someone who saw the outdoors precisely as long as it took to get indoors again. Judging from her ink-stained fingers, preferably to books, ledgers, or journals.

Not quite a librarian.

That would have been a thrill.

This finely dressed woman normally would have put a foot across a threshold by now—having not yet been let in—but the instant she thought to there, she also found reason *not* to. It vexed her.

The finely dressed woman's slightly furrowed eyebrows indicated she did not *like* being vexed.

Khumalo didn't like people with entourages, those at her doorstep especially so. "I am Khumalo," she answered.

The visitor, a pale woman under a straw hat that seemed incongruous against finery, noted that for a slender woman, the madam filled the doorway.

The visitor held a rolled certificate lightly—fingernails at each end—and wondered if her meaning had been unclear. She ran through protocol in her head: she'd knocked, announced herself, stated her intention to present a certificate of thanks (in a clear voice at a good audible level), then waited for the door to open. She had it on authority that the woman would likely be home at this hour.

Which was one hour before high noon. Feed-and-seed time, as the warehouse and dock workers liked to say. Lunch and extended bathroom use.

And it was midweek, when most errands would have already been done.

This is not to say that it had taken Mother Khumalo a long time to open the door, just that Tourmaline Dotrig had yet to embrace patience.

As Khumalo pondered, Khumalo also begrudged that, to the woman's credit, it wasn't an *entourage* but two other people who waited with the bored congenial expressions of civil servants thinking about other things they needed to do that day.

"Apologies," said Civil Servant Dotrig. "I was unclear. We have been...aware of an issue our constabulary was unable to fully grasp. And..."

This woman spoke in pauses that drove Khumalo to restrained distraction.

"...we have also noted an apparent resolution to same, brought to our attention by Mr. Stepple Grandine, first indirectly and then, at our questioning, conclusively." The sun beamed down. "Madam, may I enter?"

"Not yet."

"We do not wish to...infringe upon your talents or time, but Waterfall's had little to no crossings with magic—"

"That you're aware of," said Khumalo.

Tourmaline assented. "Of which we're aware, myself certainly not aware, which is itself a shame, as magic should be a part of everyone's allotment of fascination. To have had, as Mr. Grandine called him, a Thief Mage under our feet all these long hours is a matter of shame and security. Shame, we can forgive ourselves. Security, we can improve. On a permanent basis. If you wish."

"I have no interest in peacekeeping."

"Your actions, Madam, indicate otherwise."

"*Madam* is an honorific Stepple uses. Only him."

"We...don't know your first name. Neither does Mr. Grandine."

"It's good to see he has limits."

Tourmaline, still holding the rolled certificate, raised both hands conciliatorily. In doing so, she appeared to be presenting a scroll, which—inwardly, several levels at least—made Khumalo laugh.

"We, that is, the families and businesses of Waterfall, wanted to present you with this Certificate of Goodwill. It gets you a serving of free food at any stall, existing or new."

"Unina," said Amnandi, unseen, from behind Khumalo, "take that."

Khumalo's grin burst free. "You may enter, Madam Tourmaline of Waterfall."

**

Bog, having listened to Khumalo recount things as they sat, on a rare occasion, at Khumalo's beat-up table, weighed in: "They want you as their village witch, and they don't even know your first name. Sounds highly rewarding. The potential is staggering."

"You laugh but this is a serious matter. When a toad licks your foot some rainy night, you'll come looking for me."

"I'm not laughing. This is very serious. Do they not know you're destined for other lands? Not to sit around waiting for idiots to ward away?"

"The invitation came from the aunt of one of Amnandi's friends."

"Does the woman know this?"

"No."

"So, in a sense, her character is already of note to you. I can't imagine you not knowing the necessary details of those associated with your daughter."

"Because it would never be so. Madam Dotrig resembles her brother, the child's father. The child favors the mother. Deceased."

"The child," said Amnandi from her studies mat, "is Amis."

"And would you like to remain near Amis?" asked Khumalo.

"No, Unina. We're not done yet."

Bog did something few rarely heard: a short, loud bark of a laugh. "A true unbound spirit!"

"Had you met the aunt before?" Khumalo asked her daughter.

"No."

"What is your measure of her?"

"Wild."

"Agreed."

Bog spoke up. "Waterfall's wild minor functionaries. Perhaps this is why they take away major weapons from those entering. They don't want bloody functionary battles muddying the pathways."

Amnandi grinned and put her head back to her tablet.

Tourmaline Dotrig had been gone five hours. Bog, there for supper again, had this time cooked for them. Pressjacks and steamed jerky. The jacks had been slathered in spiced butter—a treat, he said, he'd gotten from his and Amnandi's captain herself—and which, to be honest, mother, daughter, and barbarian were now thinking of again.

Amnandi ciphered her mathematics.

Ayanda dispassionately considered options.

Bog, by will alone, held in a massive burp.

Likely for longer than he should have.

He faced Ayanda stoically.

"The muddied blood of functionaries in Waterfall will be someone else's concern, not mine," said the witch.

"I'll believe that," Bog said, standing to take his leave, "when I can walk out your door without a full stomach. Good night, Unina Khumalo."

Khumalo bowed her head. "Good night, Balagon Bog."

***

"Good morning, Madam Dotrig."

Khumalo stood before the functionary's desk.

"I have reason to believe you may wish to fortify your communal defenses. This is recent knowledge to me from a decidedly reliable source of both our acquaintance."

"Defend from whence?" said Tourmaline Dotrig.

"The mountains."

"There's nothing in the mountains."

"There's always something in mountains."

"Tales and stories," agreed Tourmaline.

"Are usually the memoirs of others. What did you know of Twitswaddle?"

"Came here. Made himself a fixture. Made himself useful. Opinions became respected, acts lauded. Tonics and bits of magic."

The noise issuing from Khumalo at "bits of magic" came as a surprise: a grunt. She didn't seem a person who contained grunts, dismissive, pained, or otherwise.

"And when people disappeared or fell rapidly into poor health?" Khumalo put. She was still standing.

"People wander. People become ill disposed toward life at times. This is a village, a large village. Constantly growing. It will need a new classification soon. Lives are not always...accounted for."

"That shall change. May I be granted an audience with the constable?"

"Are you saying you'll accept our post?"

"No, but that ignorance shall change. You are aware of Mr. Grandine because you have need for him. Same for you of me. Are you aware of Orsys, an elder who wanders from bed to bed?"

"I can't be responsible—"

"No. But are you aware?"

"I am now. I'll arrange your...audience...with the constable."

"That," said Khumalo, ending this short meeting, "is a start. I will bring information to you as it reveals itself. Twitswaddle has allies."

"He kept mostly to himself except when needed."

"As do I."

"Are you saying you're not trustworthy?"

"The lonely curry dangers. I'm not lonely." Khumalo read the sudden concern for Waterfall in Tourmaline's face. "I will report," she said to soothe her. She took her leave, stepping into the brightness of an unfettered, cloudless sky. First stop, Stepple.

***

As a young man just shy of being a fool, Stepple thought Waterfall was worth dying for. He had fallen in love several times by then, eaten lovely meals in warm homes, instinctively knew the muscles and bones of livestock and humans, and the best ways in which to plie them.

As he aged into a simple, mere "man," his beliefs in himself fell into disrepair. He made coin, but not as much as many others. He pined more than he loved. He found solace in rage so long as it was directed outward.

As a young man, he'd fought in a skirmish—nearly conscripted—off the coast of the Brints, people northward of Waterfall.

As an established man, he'd volunteered. This a war. The Brints, feeling fortified, again.

There was no longer a village of Brints.

Flowers and grasses had finally regrown on the land, though. Sailing parties kept random watch to make sure that Brint not somehow root again.

As an older man, he realized that the wars were useless, for there was plenty of coast, plenty of water, and already enough graves to fill all one's days counting, no matter where one looked.

Waterfall continued being Waterfall.

He found himself no longer in use of the Stepple he had been.

But all his life, he'd been good at listening. Old Orsys had once—when she was not old, not much older than he—told him he'd have been better picking up giving counsel rather than weapons. There was always someone needing to be talked to or, more accurately, heard, provided they were brave enough to open their mouths.

"You should have sought out bravery," she told him during the sole conversation they'd had to that point and since, at a remembrance feast of too much food, too much life wanting to be told as story, and too much wine in both of them.

"I can't turn around without the world wanting to tell me a story," he'd said, forcefully and dourly, which killed any fire Orsys might have had prior to that moment to awake with this younger man in her bed. A decade's difference of love could be taught in one night.

Twenty-five and thirty-five were but arithmetic pointing at his age now.

A lifetime of listening bearing no gain, but perhaps now bearing fruit.

"There're always stories about them what come in new," he said to Mother Khumalo as they strode a deserted alley. Morning shook off its last yawn. The midday rush would be on Waterfall soon, "Even y'self, Madam. I know what's a new lie from what's been told before. This one, this mage, came in with nothing, though, so I made sure I stayed close enough to listen. He liked to speak as if remembering things from long before anybody in the village had been born. Spoke of this as *his* place."

"Ego?"

"A lot of it. But now and then some truth. Heard it in his tone, saw it in his sadness, even though he didn't know I was listening. Massaged him now and then. Relax a body and it spills its salt. Mark, I listened most studiously those sad times. Vague talk of seeing things crushed. Vague talk of nightmares as family. Myself, I had no reason to thread it to anything till now. And same as every new face brings a tale, every old place has a legend, at least one. Generally two, though, gets you closer to the truth. There's a fable that we ran monsters away once," he said, and waited. He knew Khumalo was likely already at the end of his tale. When she waited respectfully, it gave him a burst of fire in his chest. He nodded as though she'd spoken the conclusion. "The mountains. The Great Crescent's like a snake making its way: parts of it far, parts of it near. We're a seaport. Most of the mountains is forgotten as place, history, and fables all in one."

"A fable is a story designed to teach you something."

"Only story we know is to stay home, protect Waterfall. Give it its place in the world."

He hadn't considered that Madam could look sad, but her eyes, they did something so small but steadily, he might have missed it had he not been a student of such simple things: she took him in, *all* of him, and did no more than give him space to stand upon her cupped palms. Around him, the crush of the universe, but he felt strength to push back.

"What of your place in the world?" she asked.

"I'm old, Madam. I've either forgotten it or outlived it."

She closed her eyes in a single understanding nod at him. Her scarves fluttered gently, the fins of a wonderful fish.

"Shall we meet in two days and you tell me more about fables and mountains?" she asked.

"And kin."

"And kin."

Stepple thumbed the bulb of his nose, then offered that thumb as promise to the sun. "Tomorrow, if I've any luck to me."

"Reserve your luck for your own story, not divining that of a thief unworthy to speak your name. For him, we need no more than facts. Facts are common enough."

"Yes, Madam," said Stepple, smiling a bit. He smiled more when with Mother Khumalo than he had around anyone for a long time. "Facts being common enough."

QUAKE

Waterfall had been theirs even before Waterfall had a name. Its fears, theirs to gorge on. Its larders, theirs to raid. No appetite went unsated by those who would eventually become family. Should Bash rip off a head, he regarded it as a celebration of his talons, strength, and skill. Whenever Raggle slit the throat of a night's sleep to feed on the brain seizures of the dreamer, an unwritten poem formed in the world. As for Twitswaddle, who may have been as old as the mountain—who could remember? (even Raggle had little use for history beyond fueling her rages)—Twitswaddle drank life as though wine, water, nectar or milk might never have existed.

Even how the three had converged on that spot of land by the sea was forgotten to all but the ever-watching mountains. Maybe the trees. Trees kept their own counsel, so it was difficult to tell.

Bash had been first, emerging from the sea with a dead shark slapping against his wide, rough back. Had he ever been any shade other than reptile gray, that hue was lost now. Even his chest appeared scaly, his eyes unblinking and clouded as though silt was forever added to water. Yet somehow his eyes managed to shine at night, two piercing moon-like things floating higher than could be ascribed to a great bear, let alone anything that could have been human.

Long past, his snout had caught the scent of new, unfamiliar bones.

From the sea he emerged, and by the light of their beach fire they saw his eyes and nothing more. Eyes aloft with the flat slate of night water behind.

Four people. Burly men.

All dragged snapped, cracked, twisted, and ripped back to his grotto.

They were good bones.

Bash had a sense that if he waited patiently, invisibly, more and more would come. Eventually.

A century later, the heavy, salty quickness of nightmares and fears lured Raggle from the night skies, a tattered rag given wants, talons, and teeth, jerking at the whim of air currents to land tissue-light upon the blankets of the sleeping; to skitter over their bodies, riding upward with the frenzied inhalations, spidering downward with the exhalations, across the chest, along the throat, beneath the chin, then a jump...to hover over the face. No matter how dark it was, Raggle saw the eyes wriggling under the skin. Nightmares turned the eyes into darting rats looking for escape. Raggle's own eyes were black on black and always stickily moist. When she blinked, they made sound, and that was what awoke her victims. That rhythmic reverse drip of wet flesh pulling from wet flesh.

When they opened their eyes was when Raggle, with curved claws, took hold.

When Raggle took hold, she ate.

The land, however, fed others faster. Fed livelihood. Fed hopes—be they desperate or well-founded—faster than fears. "Bodies could be buried," the land said. "Wealth will not brook as much patience as the dead do."

People kept coming.

One day, there was Twitswaddle, whose first victim was a child of twelve. Drained of spirit so fast, not even a husk formed. She became dust. That's how powerful he was then. Next, a prized bull. Then the farmer himself.

For three years, a soul a month.

For three years, hearts stopped mid-dream.

For three long years, bodies—dragged to the woods—found as mounds of flesh stripped of bones. Mangled bears found atop roofs. Skiff-sized sharks in fields.

Young Waterfall brought in magicians.

Sara, the seer, to divine the truths behind these atrocities: human, beast, or revenant?

Chate, the traveler, meant to direct the proper energies to make untoward spirits flee.

Cerece, the lightning bearer, said to be able to rend asunder with but a thought.

In the year it took to gather those three mistresses, Waterfall, ringed as it was by the Great Crescent, became a bowl of death.

The walls that had been erected and fortified time and again served only to invite Bash, Raggle, and Twitswaddle—shadows sidling beneath shadows all—to remain within.

But once the three mistresses had met, sussed out the natures of Waterfall's woes, then patiently devised a plan to grant the village its measure of peace, what to the monsters three was a brazen invitation became a thing that worried shadows beneath shadows.

The plan was a hunt.

And that was a new thing to Bash, Raggle, and Twit.

Hunted by three old women in the bright light of day and then in the spikiest parts of the prickly night. Felt out, divined, chased, set upon. All the magic within three old women brought to bear upon each demon's hungry, insatiable soul.

Cerece: burning Bash without a lick of fire to nearly a stick figure along a moonlit beach, with him only able to flee by letting his barely held-together body fall into the flat black water, using his web of grottoes and tunnels to emerge far from the people place—and perhaps days later as well; he was too pitiable to tell—where, during a night of moaning and tears, he felt a tatter of skin as ragged and torn as a death cough settle atop him and attempt to feed, but there was nothing left. So, the two lay there, not in comfort but in simply not being dead.

They awoke (not knowing when or after how long) enclosed by a rough-dug shallow trench, one muddied with water from a nearby source, and with a sharp stench of unwell urine from an even-nearer source.

Urine still *splip*ping randomly from something that had escaped a crypt so long before, it thought itself a man, body like a flailing tree branch as he coughed out words. The words meant nothing to Bash, but Raggle knew them.

Words of binding.

The witch harpy fought for consciousness, seeking the one word evil recognized amongst itself as enough reason to pause (out of curiosity if nothing else).

"Mercy..." She reached into the brain ether of the one covered by her to make its snout exhale the same appeal.

"Mur...see."

Twitswaddle continued his binding but...what was there to sup from? And how long before that witch clad all in green and gold, who had announced herself as Chate the Traveler then yanked his soul so forcibly from himself, it left his spine bowed and ribcage distended, found him? No one attacked with such force solely once and considered themselves done.

An immediate decision then.

"I bind you to my needs."

The three half-deads slithered as one toward the mountains, knowing in their deepest bones that the hunt for them was *not* over.

BAUBLES

While Ayanda observed her daughter playing with her friends, she wondered if she had laid out the best path for the two of them the best she possibly could. It wasn't a question she asked often, but she was human, and there wasn't a soul under the high moon of Sharda not meant to consider that concern.

But, Khumalo countered, who is meant to know the end of destinations? Is not any path a question solely of possibilities, not certainties?

Certainties were baubles.

Amnandi, under supervision—which entailed Mother Khumalo meditating on the grass with eyes closed and ears open— showed her friends her prowess with portals, zipping from point to point in the great expanse of wild grasses around them. None of the friends were to enter a portal, no matter if they queried, wheedled, asked openly or in secret, which of course they would all do. That directive had been explicit.

Yet the joy on Amnandi's face was as unmistakable as the fascination on the three faces watching her. Being a witch was rarely easy, usually lonely, and never stable. Her daughter's life was not easy. She deserved joy.

Amis, Khumalo noted in her meditative state, would be the first to ask her. Khumalo opened her eyes. Amis was bent low to peer as closely as she could into a wavering portal as it dissipated.

Khumalo shut her eyes.

Traveling was essential. She'd brought someone into the world; it stood to reason to show them as much of that inheritance as she could. But traveling amidst monsters, thieves, fools, and villains?

Mother Khumalo hated entertaining common thoughts that came to everyone in the night or clarity of day. For answers to those, she could ask anyone. She liked the workings of her mind cleared for things most grasped at without truly knowing what was there. The brain was a cauldron for engaging all the cosmos, not an oven for the perfunctory baking of bread.

And yet...

And yet she sat, backs of her hands lightly on her robed knees, air wafting along the scalp of her knotted hair as though in a maze, far from home, further still from returning home, and she wondered—no, hoped; no, knew; wondered if she knew; no, knew she hoped she knew--that among the many lives she could have provided for her daughter, this one offered unending joys.

She was, of course, certain her own mother, to this day, had similar thoughts about her.

Khumalo opened her eyes again in time to see Amnandi cartwheel out of a portal to masterfully (intentionally) collide with the group, nothing but laughter as they all went down.

She now found it pleasurable to meditate with eyes open.

Tomorrow, an audience with the constable.

***

Constable Bethune was precisely the type of person who should have retired before he took the job. Everything from his loose posture to his uniform being crisp enough but not crisp, spoke of a soul mired by duty upon duty upon duty.

"Soft about the jowls" described him perfectly. In all aspects of his life.

Definitely.

Khumalo wound not pity him.

She had been in his office less than five minutes and already wished to take her leave of him.

"Were you aware of citizens, primarily women, falling prey?" said Khumalo.

"People fade every single day, Miss."

"So I've heard. I was not so long ago acquainted with someone in your line of work. She is as tall as I, hair as red as bleeding. They called her the Red Constable. She had the unearned reputation of having killed a fae. No one in this realm has that capability. Yet she never so much as raised her voice to maintain order. The village of Kettedge. Do you know it?"

"It's barely a hamlet. Waterfall is at least ten times its size."

"Then your citizens should expect ten times more vigilance from you. She knew the names of everyone in her care. You do not strike me as having decided to make that effort. Not an insult, a suggestion. You'll find benefits."

"Tell me again why we're meeting?"

"I am assessing options should a need arise."

"And—and," he said, mimicking her, yet with care, "no insult given—you are? Miss Dotrig told me to expect you. Beyond that,

I'm not sure of the purpose of our chat."

"I am possibly the person who saves your life. I've assessed enough. Madam Dotrig will inform you of me further. Thank you, Constable Bethune."

For the second time in as many days, she left someone befuddled at their desk as she stepped into a bright day's sun.

***

It was Orsys's turn to worry about this woman named Khumalo. Wonder? Worry? At Orsys's age, it didn't seem there was much of a difference between the two words, seeing that whatever the circumstance, her wavering mind would be of no assistance.

But the young one respected her, so Orsys made sure to recall her name at least once per hour. Perhaps there was magic given in that act of making someone real.

She'd seen the young one stepping lively that day from the porches of official offices, and official was never a good thing. A bad thing for a citizen, doubly so for a stranger in stranger lands. She had yet to see Khumalo purchase a single thing she didn't need—and Waterfall had more of such things than tree needles—or spend an inordinate amount of time somewhere making sure she was seen spending that inordinate amount of time.

Which was called *leisure*.

There'd been more people coming from the southern coasts and inland west for fungible quality. She knew *fungible*; she'd been a teacher much loved by her students even as they aged. Leisure. She never thought she'd live to see the day when leisure, being a matter of hard travel and significant sums of money, became more work than work.

No, official is what leisure became, which didn't seem right in any way. Khumalo, the tall woman made of petrified wood and sunrise; liked her from the moment she saw her. Energy that wasn't so much kind as right.

The tall woman made of petrified wood and sunrise felt right.

Which was another reason to worry/wonder. Nothing right ever came out of official. The two didn't match. Official was concerned with never becoming unofficial, not with what was right.

Ayanda Khumalo. The woman had gifted her her full name.

Orsys Major, Orsys had responded. At least, she might have. She hoped she had.

She decided, as she now watched Khumalo make her subtle beeline for the nearest sweetbread stall, that she had.

Orsys left the crate set out for her by the salted-fish woman inland from the harbor (sister of the fresh-fish woman, first stall along the shoppers' pier) and walked the same direction Khumalo walked, making note of Stepple asleep on the ground at the fringes. It didn't matter which fringe; people would've found it odd for Stepple to *not* be at a fringe.

She was older than him but he generally moved older than her, and that was entirely because some tended to be stupid with their lives, burning their stock of resources such as health and welfare as though utterly replenishable.

Which they weren't. Not for anyone. Not even for those who did good in the world. She hadn't met many people who moved as though they were made of sun and rock, so Orsys's soul knew to gravitate toward one when she did. She had enjoyed teaching history the most, which—when lucid enough in life's current forgetfulness to appreciate irony—was about keeping a record of why people should be allowed to remain on the goddess's lifegiving teat.

A record, then, of being cared for despite evidence to the

contrary.

Like a filing trailing a lodestone, Orsys made sure to keep her record of rocks and suns in sight. Khumalo walked as slowly as she did, and during frequent pauses to study some small thing or plant herself on the fringes to listen to someone tout new wares to travelers who'd gathered around, Orsys was permitted to rest, always just enough to begin to follow anew.

There was something troublesome in the air. Orsys could feel it trying to worm inward whenever she took a breath. Her mind's eye—had she believed in such—saw it as a tattered fog around Khumalo but never quite touching the woman. Whether not touching out of fear or lack of strength was unsure. But it, too, followed Khumalo like a lost bit of metal to a lodestone.

That would not do.

If Orsys remembered anything clearly, it was that she protected those in search of the renewal of good things.

***

For a brusque-but-effective way of nudging him that things were afoot, Orsys stepped on Stepple.

"What's on with you, old mum! Do you not see?" cried Stepple. Orsys continued on precisely as if she neither saw nor felt him. He was about to shout "Hey now!" but he knew that particular follow, a combination of focusing on several things at once: stealth, intention, and determination. Not to be interrupted.

But certainly to be observed. Khumalo herself had passed this way only minutes before. She'd been some distance across the hardpacked dirt of Vendors' Row. He caught glimpses of her scarves stitching in and out of the growing crowds while he pretended to sleep against the side of a public loo. The day was warm and comfortable, though, the breeze off the water cool and insistent, meaning he wouldn't put lie to it and say there wasn't more sleep in this nap than pretend.

The Row was large and a nap easily shaken from; his eye on things might close, but his ears remained ready and alert.

He'd been dreaming. It had been a good dream, one that felt just pleasurable enough for him to overlook his circumstances.

Until she stepped on him.

Though she was old, her eyesight was as keen as anyone else's. His leg protruded outward with purpose; it announced him. As he pulled the leg inward, someone who had observed his pain tossed the smallest coin in their purse his way while continuing on their own. He pocketed it without taking an eye off either Orsys or Khumalo.

Khumalo, on the opposite side of the Row, perhaps a hundred or so good steps away, stood paused at a graybeet stand. He knew for a fact Madam did not like graybeets.

Orsys, once beautiful Orsys, once vibrant Orsys, still beautiful Orsys and—each time he recalled a brief moment of potential desire—still vibrant, moving in such a way as to get from place to place without anyone seeing her walking until she wanted them to. What was it Madam had said to him when he wondered if there was room for magic in the world?

"There's magick all around."

"It doesn't need us to see it," she'd said, and he'd understood: it simply does what it does.

Orsys wore a set of her summer rags but in a new way. Colors were out of sync but varied. Red atop brown, a green length of fabric tying a threadbare yellow wrap to her. Her crinkly gray hair was unadorned, but on her feet, a black sandal and an orange sandal.

One rainbow trailing another.

And he all in gray.

When both women put enough distance and crowd between him to be out of his sight, Stepple ended his "nap" for a walk in their general direction. It was a good day for such a walk.

***

She retrieved the scroll of provision from the loose sleeve of her robe several times to procure goods, but no one saw her carry a thing. Of course, sweetbreads. And fruit, several new varieties fresh (as fresh as possible) from the southernmost of the southern coasts. Spices, dried fish, cured meat, small squares of fabric said to have been blessed by one of the many intercessional deities in this land who seemed to bless anything set before them. Each stall had a ready-made story for the high-quality-yet-exceedingly-affordable items offered. The cloth was said to have come from the notable Captain Pinyasama's last trip herself. Bog had not mentioned magical cloth among the ship's catch; Khumalo would have to badger him on the efficacy of giving a full report, preferably to make him laugh during a sparring session, thereby throwing him off balance and thereby unprepared for a new offensive she'd been considering.

She made a mental note to find something here he'd like.

Two stalls down, she found it. A fur loincloth that looked as if the animal it came from still lived there. The wooly thing had the unmitigated gall to have matching boots.

"Winters come quick here, missus," said the grizzled stallkeeper.

"Yes," agreed Khumalo, "but...surely, there's more to it? Who would wear such in winter?" Her mind was already made up to purchase the set, but this mirth was too heady to neglect.

"It's the style," he yammered. "I won't pretend to fathom the barbarian mind."

"I imagine they're full of mischief."

"Mischief, missus? What of murder?"

"Not as much as you'd think." She gauged boot and loincloth size. "Those, if I may. Is there at least a cloak?"

"Next week, a shipment for certain."

She paid, had him twine them in a bundle, carried them off, then—perhaps no more than thirty steps back along the way she'd come, her business done—greeted Orsys, hands free.

"Good day to you, beloved," said Khumalo. Orsys nodded, body bowed more than usual, breathing slightly labored. "Are you tired? Shall we sit?" Khumalo moved toward a splintered table and equally worn bench. Whereas during the day's walk, Khumalo existed on the fringes, she now parted crowds as per usual. She waited for Orsys to catch up. When the elder did, there was a loaf of sweetbread awaiting in its opened cloth. When, with a *whump*, Orsys sat, Khumalo broke the bread into threes. Orsys ate quietly, pausing now and then to shine her eyes at the milling throngs.

Her eyes lighted on Stepple at the same time Khumalo's did.

"Friend," said Khumalo, whose pointing out the bread with a wave was an entire conversation.

Stepple approached and sat. He reached for the bread. Orsys stayed his hand with a gentle tap, saying to Khumalo, "What of the small one?"

Khumalo smiled. "I have plenty."

Orsys nodded at Stepple.

"Would either of you care for water?" asked Khumalo.

Both nodded, Orsys staring at a pattern of wood on the table, Stepple around a mouthful of dry bread.

"I believe I saw a rain barrel nearby," said Khumalo.

"You've no cups," said Stepple.

"I have cups."

Khumalo returned with two cups of clear water. Stepple noted appreciatively there were no leaves, bugs, or sediment.

Khumalo broke off a hunk of her portion and savored every chew of it. When done, she took a deep breath, let the exhalation wander, and told the two of them, "I am having a good day." She lifted a hand to the crowd. "So many needs and wants joined together in a nearly physical manifestation. This is the first I've experienced it this way."

"*Poverty makes people happy* was the slogan of one of our largest merchants," said Stepple. "Had a huge share of the Warehouse. Dead now. Mysterious circumstances."

"Mysterious circumstances," Orsys chorused.

"*Coins leaving pockets*. He was a huge proponent of that. Coins leaving pockets was a form of community mindfulness."

"I imagine his coins were dispersed to the community for maximum joy?" said Khumalo.

"Nah," said Stepple. "Wife. Son. They hold it quite well."

"Peckers," said Orsys.

Stepple hooked a thumb at the old woman. "Precisely what she said. Every other person in that crowd's a pecker too. Unless *pecker*'s something good to you?"

"Not particularly."

"A good day's not to be tossed, though. We're glad of it." He caught Orsys sliding a portion of bread into a fold of clothing, and followed her wise lead. "And young madam is well?"

"She is."

"What of the brute?" barked Orsys.

"The brute abides."

"Bog the Unsmiling! Who calls themselves that?" said Stepple.

"He doesn't."

Stepple frowned. "I wager he wouldn't need to, with his thighs and sinew and whatnot."

"Biceps. Massive," said Orsys.

"He is well," Khumalo declared, snipping that line of thought.

Stepple, his back to the sea, looked off into the distance, eyes roving over the Great Crescent's contours. "The Bite's looking peaceful."

Khumalo looked over her shoulder at it. It did indeed look as though a behemoth had leapt from beneath the horizon to snap a bite out of the foolishly dangling sky.

"Have you been to the mountains?" asked Khumalo.

"Once," said Stepple. "Nothing there beyond huffy deer, gruff goats, and hares with malice in their eyes toward trespassers."

Orsys had begun her withdrawal. Khumalo stretched forward and laid soft fingertips atop the back of the elder's inactive hand as Orsys's left absently shuttled bits of bread to her mouth. "Tell us of your travels, dear one."

Rather than a trickle, the bursting of a dam. "I saw the hoof of a unicorn; was iridescent. Sailed to Afrela and back. There's a statue that comes to life in Vaalwud. As a young woman, I fell in love with two separate demons each time I bathed in a certain stream—no, young Stepple, I will not tell you where—and each tried to love me more than the other. I tried to get to Nosk, but people kept telling me it didn't exist even though I knew they'd been there. There was once"—Orsys stopped to think—"that I taught a child queen to print her name in all the alphabets of her land." She frowned deeply. "I don't remember where and I should, because she made an edict that I should only eat desserts while there. She wanted me to be happy." She looked directly into Khumalo's eyes. "I should remember where."

"You will," promised Khumalo.

"I worried about you this morning, so I made sure the paths you took were safe ones. I've thought about walking to the mountains some morning. Find a cave. Go to sleep. Disappear."

"From all records," Khumalo said.

"From all records." Orsys closed her eyes, only to quickly open them when she felt Khumalo's long, strong, fingers squeeze her hand.

"Not all," said Khumalo.

To Stepple's astonishment, Orsys laid a hand atop Khumalo's. Orsys never touched anyone anymore, not if it could be helped.

It was that precise moment that respect for Madam became love, and Stepple Grandine was an expert in undying love. "I sadly confess I've not had the luck I'd hoped regarding our business," he said.

"I am confident you will. For now, we've the luck of an agreeable day and magnificent sweetbread. Will that do this table of champions for a little while?"

"It'll do," said Stepple.

Orsys nodded. "It's doing."

"Then neither of us need do more outside of leaving enough crumbs for mice."

"To the mice of Waterfall," said Stepple, clay mug raised to the sky before he drained it in three big gulps. "They be slight but they be many and quick."

"And thus?" said Khumalo.

"They be strong." He touched his head and heart to her as he had seen Bog do. She returned the gesture.

All sat a bit longer under an agreeable sun until Orsys wandered away. A pang hit Stepple in the heart. He sniffed brusquely to hide it. "The mice of Waterfall," he said. His eyes swung to Khumalo's. "Loves of lives. Dreams...gone. Gone in wars. Gone in just having to wake up." Maybe it was Orsys's opening herself up; maybe all that spirit suddenly leaking from her affected him. He didn't want to speak but he wouldn't stop, and it seemed Khumalo was there to listen. "You ever stab someone, mum? It's a feeling that never leaves your hands." He held his upward as though she were to examine them. "A sword's no better than a knife. It's just killing someone at a distance from you so's you can see the life leave them better. All we try to do in this world is slice off a bit of each other. I don't like that, mum. Pardon. Madam."

Khumalo waited until he returned his hands to the table.

"I will not kill," she said. "And nor will you lament love when it lives and breathes mere paces from you. Orsys would not have sat at this table if she didn't consider you worthy. You do know that?"

"I suppose I needed a reminder, mum. Sorry, Madam."

"*Mum* will do for now."

After several quiet moments, they left the table, walked in tandem for a bit, then parted.

GROWING

For most of the farmers, the last of the summer harvests were coming in for sale to travelers before traveling tapered off. Around the temptations of fruits and vegetables nearly bursting with sugars, children were more hindrance than help. A week was always set aside at the beginning of the final harvest for all children under the age of thirteen to be chore-free (outside of the regular chores of cleaning or upkeep).

Amis took full advantage of this week, leading her band a little deeper into the woods each day.

The girl had what Mother Khumalo called a "fervor" to her, and Amnandi had been charged by Mother to keep watch on the spry, wild, smiling girl's behalf.

This was the fourth day of that week, three days after Unina's shopping excursion.

Amis was trapped in a tree.

Firstly, she'd climbed too high.

Secondly, the branch between the one she was on and the one she needed to reach in order to lower herself no longer existed, as it had snapped, then broken into numerous wood shards on the way down.

Thirdly—and this was the second time Amnandi had said this toward that high point in the tree—"Children are annoying!" It wasn't that she couldn't portal up there to get her (she could), but she didn't want to have to use magick for foolishness.

Bettany and Gita hadn't arrived yet.

Amnandi had noted the number of branches cracked at the base of the tree and had warned that this tree wasn't suitable for climbing.

"I know that," said Amis, shimmying up the narrow trunk for a low-hanging limb. "We call this 'Knucklebones' for the way twigs look when they break off." All around the tree: knucklebones.

She'd known...and had continued to climb.

Amnandi knew if Gita and Bettany were with them, Amis wouldn't have climbed, but alone—and clearly, the girl thought of herself as alone when with Amnandi—risks demanded to be taken.

Amnandi gritted her teeth, threw the portal, exited it on the branch Amis waited upon, yanked Amis in just as the first *crack* of that branch sounded, and threw another to land them a good distance away from that particular copse of trees lest Amis consider this a new game.

Amnandi walked a few steps, fully expecting a stream of excitable utterances from her wee friend, but Amis was silent behind her. Amnandi turned.

She had never met anybody for whom the term "wild eyes" really applied, but, clearly, Amis couldn't speak because all of her concentration was focused there. Then a bit of it trickled to her smile. Then entire face and mouth.

"It feels like puppy lightning!" Amis broke forth. "I'm tingly and full of wind."

"Ha, yes, you are," said Amnandi, having learned fart humor from Amis herself.

"I love that you can do that, how do you do that, teach me to do it, can we do it all the time?"

Amnandi, hoping to lead by example, accordioned her rump to the ground and pretended interest in the nearly physical rays of light piercing the jangly fingers of reaching trees like perfectly thrown javelins.

"Will you get in trouble if you show me?"

This was an intriguing thought. Amnandi had never thought of magick in terms of teaching. Her only experience was in learning. Yet in learning, there was a teacher...

She would have to ask Unina about this.

But for now, silence.

"You're not talking. Are you mad?" said Amis.

"No."

Amis circled her and then sat beside her. "I climb Knucklebones all the time."

"Your aunt visited my home."

"Did she?"

"Yes."

"She does that. Important stuff. Your ma's important. I like your ma."

Amnandi nodded.

"She like me?"

Amnandi nodded.

Amis brightened. "I'm glad she's here."

"We won't be forever."

"Till you do, we're sisters," said Amis.

"I think we'll be sisters forever, but you have to stay out of trees."

"You mean don't be foolish? Like I'm a child?"

"A foolish child."

"I," said Amis with authority, "have energy. Auntee told me." She paused to consider. "Is magic energy?"

"In a way."

"So, I could be a great magician!"

"Likely destruction," said Amnandi.

"You're my sister because you don't call me 'Empty.'"

"Empty?"

'My mid name's Emty," Amis explained, then spelled it.

"I didn't know that. How do you know I won't call you 'Empty' now?"

"You won't."

"Do our other sisters?"

"They used to. Gita did. Bettany just once. You got a mid?"

"No."

"Amnandi Khumalo," Amis said, rolling the syllables along her tongue. "I like that. Feels powerful."

Amnandi touched her own forehead, then completed the circuit by tapping Amis's in thanks.

"Bettany and Gita are nearby," said Amnandi.

"You can tell?"

Amnandi nodded.

The tips of the Great Crescent were visible between branches from their angle. Amis spied glances at it fairly frequently.

"What fascinates you about that range?" asked Amnandi.

"It's far away. It's adventure." The answer, however, rang lifeless. "How far can we go in one of those airholes?"

This was another thing Amnandi had never considered. Learning was a thing done in stages, never limit to limit.

"I'm sure none of our parents would be happy at the prospect of us in the mountains," said Amnandi.

"I'm not interested in my Da's happiness, he's had long enough to find it, and you're a granny in a tiny body."

"I'm very interested in Unina's."

Footsteps atop knucklebones, then shuffling through dry grass, followed by voices announced the arrival of Bettany and Gita.

"Isn't there anything you want to do for yourself?" Amis quickly asked before Gita and Bettany slalomed between trunks into view a moment later.

"Why are you so far out here?" asked Gita, ever the practical elder.

"How'd you find us?" Amis asked.

"You're loud enough to wake bones," said Gita.

"No burials around here," said Amis.

"There's bones everywhere," said Gita. Bettany, for her part, was enrapt of a red butterfly in her palm and left words to the others.

"Can you conjure bones from the ground?" Amis asked Amnandi.

"That would be foolish and rude even if I could," said Amnandi, standing to peruse the beauty in Bettany's hand. A red jewel with brown spots, unbothered and unhurried.

"But you haven't said you can't," Gita pointed out.

"Auntee says you'll make an outstanding administrator," Amis told Gita.

"I can't," said Amnandi.

"Magic is odd," said Amis.

"Amis still wants to go to the mountains," said Amnandi.

"There's nothing there, Amis," said Gita.

"But do you have proof?" Amis said, peering intently for her friend's answer, intensity which went utterly disregarded.

Gita, kneeling, carefully emptied a rucksack. "No Death and the Farmer today. My da lent me his science tools." At her knees: a magnifying glass, a telescope, a water finder, and a set of long, fine-tipped tongs. Amnandi instantly went for the magnifying glass.

"Are witches allowed to do science?" asked Amis.

"It's all we do," said Amnandi, regarding the butterfly with the glass, careful to keep any sun away.

"We won't wander deeper into the wood," Gita announced.

Amis grabbed up the telescope, training it toward the mountains. High, puffy clouds floated serenely over the range as though nothing but dreams and sky existed there.

"Amis..." said Gita.

"It's not dark and there's nothing else to see! Leave me alone."

"Bettany?" said Gita. "Finder or tongs?"

"Nothing for me," said Bettany, nearly entranced by the butterfly's languid movements.

Gita gathered the remaining items before wordlessly leading the exploration party back toward their horses and usual meeting grounds. There were numerous stops to look at bugs, bark, mushrooms, and moss.

It was lost on none of them that Amis kept training the scope on the mountains. Fortunately, the mountains were too far away for her to be a trouble concerning them.

***

How far could she go?

The morning's play was done, noon's learning understood, and Unina off in the village again. Mother had asked if she wanted to attend with her but, truly, if Amnandi weren't going on a ship with Bog again, the village held little interest.

The afternoon was bright, Amnandi's inner sightline clear, her sense of herself and her selves nicely aligned, and the meditation she had completed moments before (consisting of only two words: *I go*) left such clarity, she felt she'd matured ten years.

Portals were line-of-memory-sight, connecting her from where she knew she'd been to where she decided to go. She was expert at rapid-fire hops. Could even easily go from the home, which was where she was, to the meeting-place clearing, which she didn't consider far at all.

She studied the mountains in the distance.

Because they were so far away, they looked painted rather than real, but she was acquainted with that illusion. Distant things wanted you to come to them, so they made themselves dreamlike. In this way, people were made pollinators, except instead of propagating pollens, they spread reality, for a place never fully existed until experienced. The more experiences, the more real.

Amnandi focused. Exhaled herself into the throwing of her portal. Entered without hesitation. Immediately felt something was not right. The experience of a portal was as a rushing wind at her back. This time, with the mountain range clearly in mind, there was an accompanying wind in front of her, effectively sandwiching her into a slowed state of nothingness, panicking her just for a moment out of surety and into one of the emergency states Unina had taught her.

Amnandi Green, in exactly the same spot Amnandi had previously left her, same posture, clothing and demeanor as well, watched her pop in, Green's expression immediately concerned.

Amnandi had a look of uncertainty she rarely had, and this wasn't even an uncertainty of the type to be figured out.

This was fear.

"What's wrong?"

Amnandi couldn't answer a second. The frown on her face was ten years older, born prematurely of concerns she should not have had.

"Ai!" Green called like a finger snap.

"Trying something new," Amnandi said. "It didn't work. I'm glad you're here."

"Can you get home?

Amnandi nodded.

"Good. Go home and go home quickly. I can tell when you're not here by choice."

Amnandi needed something to ground her. She took Green's hands in hers and suddenly asked something she'd never asked. "Do you go away when I'm not here?"

"You never leave here," said Green.

Amnandi nodded, took a calming breath, and showed herself the strength she needed to see by stepping back, releasing Green's brown hands, and quickly parting the veil between their worlds. Back into herself, she emerged from that particular between to the grass behind her home, exactly where she'd started. She threw three consecutive portals, one taking her to the Knucklebone tree, one to a stream she and Unina liked to visit far past the village road, and the last—for sheer spite—to a large burnt spot in the woods even farther away.

It was where she and Unina had once lived.

Nothing had survived the flames. The enduring odor of ash mixed with rain mixed with renewing dirt rooted her to the spot. Even the metal stove was gone, yet of course, metal was too precious to leave unclaimed.

Amnandi could still picture the two foolish children playing with her outside it.

Amnandi felt tired more tired than she thought she ought to be. Her fingertips, forehead, and toes tingled, whereas her midsection felt numb. Her breathing came in and out overly calm, and this was how she knew her automatic self had temporarily taken up post.

She wanted to sit. Her auto self wouldn't allow it. She felt tears coming; auto allowed them unhindered. Not full tears as Amis or Bettany might shed. These were stinging tears that pooled along the rim, never falling, instead performing a kind of science with the air to become acid.

This patch of char had been a home, one of the first they'd had in Eurola until the night they fled it.

"*The air in my house tastes like sugar*," she had said to the girl of her age, Greta, and her rotund, blond, younger brother. Unina had allowed them in to play. Amnandi, now considering herself a child then, although it was but months back, showed them everything, including veils. A veil in the oven to another world.

The terrified boy had cried all the way home.

The neighboring hamlet deemed the tall woman and her quiet child dangerous.

Amnandi had learned that people in this cloudy land used danger as excuse for brutal decisions.

A little house in the woods. Burned all the way down after the citizenry were sure the inhabitants had fled.

Amnandi's chin touched her chest. She suddenly did not want to go any farther. She threw a portal, only one, from there to what, for convenience's sake, was called home.

***

Unina Khumalo, arriving at the shack, immediately held her daughter's face and kissed her forehead, and laid her own forehead to hers for a moment, then had her help prepare the root vegetables for soup later. "Bog will not be joining us," Khumalo informed. "He said he has to prepare for a journey."

Amnandi's eyes shot wide.

"He will not leave without seeing you," her mother reassured. "Mind your knife."

Amnandi minded the knife, but every bit of her also wanted to *change* something. Two things not feeling right in quick succession left knots where knots were not wanted. The misshapen tuber in her hand, no matter how precisely sliced, would never have answers for her, nor the knife—an heirloom from her grandmother, as beautiful with its hilt carvings as anything made purely for pleasure—it would never change anything vital. Mundane things did nothing, while people and homes came and went.

"A witch with nothing more to say on an important matter vexes me," said Khumalo. "You have nothing further to say?"

The problem was too much to say without the vocal space in her throat to say it.

"Breathe," said Mother Khumalo.

Amnandi spaced her breaths at either side of the knife strokes until the sensation of tingling went away. After that, just the rhythmic *plok* of the blade against the wooden board counted moments in the small home.

"Unina..." Even that word made her want to cry now.

Khumalo sipped the seasoned broth. "Shhh. Speak only when you are ready."

"Thank you."

"I will not need to go into the village tomorrow. What shall we do? Think on it."

And in that small home with doors and shutters open for breezes morning to night, the *plok plok plok* of a knife served to do what it, and only it, could do.

***

Amnandi refused to be afraid of what she could not do. That kept the sweat away from her eyes. It was a hot day, even for what she was used to considering hot. The usual breeze circulating the bowl of the Great Crescent and its footlands had gone flat.

I am in good company if winds have to deal with fears too, she thought, focusing intensely on Unina's words:

"Thought, time, and place are inseparable, my sweet," said Unina Khumalo. "They are of one accord."

"The way I am not separated from my selves."

"*You* are all you. Thought begins all. Thought becomes memory. Memory becomes time. Time becomes place. That is your meditation. Please repeat it, beginning with 'Memory becomes time.'"

"Memory becomes time. Time becomes place."

"When you have been to a place, you remain in that place. Repeat."

"When you have been to a place, you remain in that place." Amnandi ignored the sweat along her brow. She kept her eyes closed but inner eyes open. Unina had told her to picture the dock that had received the ship she and Bog had voyaged upon.

"When I tap your back," Khumalo said out of view behind Amnandi, "I want you to get there a moment before I do."

A touch of tingling again. Amnandi had never attempted a portal in a densely populated area.

Mother Khumalo read her hesitation. "It is quite early. There will be very few there."

This felt very much different from a line-of-sight portal. "What happens if someone is in the same space as a portal?"

"A portal's energies naturally avoid those of souls. To connect otherwise would have to be an intentional act."

"It sounds...unfortunate in its intention."

"We are not weapons, child."

"Memory becomes time. Time becomes place," Amnandi murmured.

"Realization becomes path." She tapped Amnandi's back.

The child threw the portal and disappeared.

In the split second of *between*, only the wind at her back.

Khumalo threw her own portal and exited to see her daughter gazing enrapt at the sea.

Huge ships slept moored so they wouldn't wander or perhaps dream so deeply that they went under. Although Amnandi knew ships didn't dream. Unina had given her the word for imagining so: *anthropomorphize*. To offer crumbs of life to the inanimate in hopes they take it.

"Knowing where you need to go takes away all fear," said Mother Khumalo.

"Is that why we travel as we do, by foot and horse and ship, so we can return in our own way?"

"Partly."

"How far can we go? Home?" said Amnandi, meaning the warm, life-filled grasses of the Afrelan cities they knew.

Khumalo pointed to Erah's moon, still slightly visible in the post-dawn sky. "Perhaps someday we'll go to her, to Sharda herself."

"First with a balloon," Amnandi said smiling.

"On the winds of a monsoon."

"Minding not to crash in a lagoon."

"Would be inopportune."

"We'd take a good ladder to the moon."

"Why?"

"So we wouldn't be marooned."

Khumalo smiled widely at her small one, who was not, in truth, so small. "You, my sweet, will be the first to whistle a tune on Sharda, our spying moon. How do you feel?"

"A little tired."

"Your stamina will increase. Travel across great distances extracts energy directly from the brain."

"I have a big head."

"Perfect for storing all the experiences yet to come. Home now."

Dock stragglers saw two portals form, a woman and child enter them, the woman and child disappear.

Magic had returned to Waterfall.

***

There were those who attended public meetings solely to reinforce their penchant for being nuisances. The cramped public-inquiry space had once been a tiny schoolhouse during Waterfall's less-populated days. It retained its rows of bench seating, although now raised to accommodate adult cogitations. "We have never had a village sorcerer," a current nuisance, Kieran Horne of the Property Guild, said, "let alone a witch. A foreign witch," he added to bolster what he considered was a point.

Kieran Horne made it his business to attend any and all public forums, bleating for accountability everywhere but in his own ledgers. He financed three stalls along Vendors' Row.

Tourmaline Dotrig, of course, hated public forums as any good administrator would, preferring to be getting things actually done rather than hear out half-formed thoughts that barely qualified as opinions.

"We have never needed it," said Tourmaline, wondering again how it wasn't the village leaders at these meetings but her, meant to report back *to* the village leaders.

"And we do not officially need it now," said Constable Bethune.

"But we've legitimate concerns."

"Of what nature?" said Kieran. "When's the last even a sprite was hereabouts?"

"There's been official jurisprudence business," said Bethune, "that points toward the unseen world."

"You love your own voice too much, Bethune. Your aim to keep that world unseen with monies from our pockets?"

Tourmaline, seated on a barstool behind a lectern, said, "A stipend would be respectful toward a witch's time."

"Where's the respect for us?" said Kieran. "I expect she'll come in *doing* things. I don't approve."

"Mr. Horne, you are an esteemed representative of the Property Guild but you are *not* the Property Guild. A proper vote will be held."

"I'd think—"

"Do be quiet." Tourmaline's patience was exhausted by fools. She nodded at Constable Bethune to continue.

"As I understand things," said the constable, "there could be danger coming from the Crescent."

"Sorcerer goats," Kieran huffed, being sure to laugh at his own joke so fellow guildspeople would know to laugh too.

Tourmaline strode from the lectern to stand over him. "We had in our midst a mage stealing lives. Twelve known at current assessment and who knows how many before the enterprise was thwarted. Some appeared as sicknesses; others we've no trace of. I've had Constable Bethune going through death records for this year. He is none too happy about that, but he is halfway through the task because—tell me why, constable."

"I does my job."

"He does his job. You and I have done this dance, Mr. Horne, and I would have hoped by now, you'd find the steps boring. Mr. Robison, are you taking down every word of this for dissemination?" she said toward a quiet gentleman with a handlebar mustache that twitched in rapid concentration at the back of the room.

"I am," he said, adding *I am* to an official Waterfall note-taking notebook.

Tourmaline speared Horne with her attention again. "This is a serious matter, yet you insist on being disruptive minus any point. A deputy will remove you at the next outburst. Constable Bethune, do we have a deputy eager for this?"

"Deputy Cooney at the door, ma'am," said Bethune, "has learned a new method of requesting cooperation."

Deputy Cooney stood five feet tall but when straightened at attention (as now) was easily six She gave a tip of the head to Horne.

"This is a public meeting, miss," said the irritant.

"Exactly," said Tourmaline. "You are the public...and I am the official. One of us is tasked to be of use; the other isn't. A very easy guess which. Despite the open forum and despite the requisite vote, this matter will come to bear. Would you care to see a body I had exhumed as part of my duties? I thought not."

"Looked as a gourd left in the sun, all the seeds and innards dried out," said the constable. "Her family buried her quick for fear of a new disease."

Kieran gave a glance to Deputy Cooney. "And it's magics because a gaudily dressed traveler says it's magics? She who has everything to gain while presenting no proof?"

"You'll weep the day you meet someone you trust, Mr. Horne," said Tourmaline. She took her place behind the lectern again. "Take this information to your guilds. Let them know of our intentions and the reason thereof. We reconvene in two days to ratify."

Robison and his team distributed transcripts the following

day: tacked to the village's five public posts, hand-delivered to all guild houses.

By the second day, there may have been three or five people not talking about the witch of Waterfall and the Thief Mage purported to be at their door.

Even those who had not seen Mother Khumalo knew the witch was her when they saw her.

After being assured by Bog that he would be back, Amnandi— needing diversion from any possible cloudy thoughts—had requested a field trip for her day with her mother. One including her friends. The inclusion of friends delayed things, such that seeing Ayanda Khumalo striding even more through the village could not be helped. The robed and scarfed woman had thought to borrow additional science equipment from Gita's father, who informed her and Amnandi that with permission for his daughter to go on the trip, others wanted to go too. It was children's week off for summer harvest, and word from children traveled faster than a sneeze. The same from Amis and Bettany's weary parents.

The following day, Khumalo and Amnandi rode into the village with Beedma, Natuun, and parcel sacks over each steed.

They rode out, to the murmurings and starings of many, with a train of children on various pack animals following them, including a very small giddy child on a goat.

The village had a new protector of children, also of people in general. And one parent's permission wouldn't be shown to show up another's.

Thus Mother Khumalo led her first group field trip ever. With her daughter at the fore, she rode out of Waterfall, past her home, and into the familiar yet new woods for what, as far as the children were concerned, was already a great day.

***

Mother Khumalo had quickly identified each by trait.

One was unruly due to lack of attention.

One was loud to mark her place in a big family.

One's curiosity kept them quietly fascinated by all things. Khumalo could tell they contained many like Amnandi did.

The sullen child had not expanded his vocabulary to encompass his love of life.

Gita, Amnandi, and Bettany weaved in and out among them all, at turns students, at turns teachers.

And Amis, whom Khumalo secretly admired, was Amis.

The group, however, was now scattered, both in focus and location.

Khumalo clapped her hands sharply, which let out a *crack* as though a tree branch had struck brittle ice. "Today," she said into the resulting silence, "we are dragoons. When I need you to attend, I'll call 'dragoons!' And you will?"

"Gather!" shouted the wee quiet one of many souls, who had ridden there on a goat. They were, Khumalo estimated, eight.

"And you will also?"

"Listen!" shouted the loud one, barely bigger than the wee one despite being the same age as Amnandi and Bettany.

"Excellent. Amnandi and Amis may also call out 'dragoons!' Should they do so, attend." Khumalo softened her bearing just enough for the children to drop out of rigid attention. "Resume explorations. And put nothing in your mouths. Including frogs, no matter what they say."

The group quickly and communally considered this last statement. Coming from the Witch of Waterfall, talking frogs might very well have been something they'd all missed before.

Instant expansion.

Amnandi and Amis took to their deputization with grace,

pointing out the fascinating bits of this part of the forest they frequented, with the unspoken agreement that they would someday visit the parts the other children favored.

The beaches were fun in their way, but a forest would always present a full invitation.

Eight youngsters sought things they had not seen before.

Amis found a trove of gray slugs. Amnandi noticed. "Dragoons!" Amnandi shouted. Six bodies trotted from here and there, kneeling to peer under the lightweight rotting log Amis kept raised.

"Slugs," Amnandi announced, "like ale."

"You mean like in the rowdy barn? Regular ale?"

"Are they sad?" asked the wee goat-rider.

"Chemicals," said Amnandi. "The ale is like dead soup: decaying sweets and yeasts."

"Yeast is baking," said the unruly one who had yet to act out.

"Yeast is everywhere," said Amnandi. "Everything is everywhere."

"Even fire?" piped the Wee again.

"In a way. Unina always reminds me to keep in mind an important word: *potential*. There's potential for fire in everything."

"I want to draw out the fire," said Wee.

"Not here," interjected Amis.

"Why?"

"It's a forest." Amis angled the log higher. Larger slugs clung to the bottom of it. Smaller ones sought crevices in the damp earth in refuge from this prolonged sudden breath of wind.

"Too much potential?" said Wee.

Amis nodded at them with a smile.

"Bugs get drunk!" said the unruly boy. His name was Nate.

"Where do they get ale out here?" said the quiet-up-to-now loud child.

"Probably fairy parties," said Unruly Nate boisterously.

"Beetle bartenders!"

"Slugs as tired das and mas!"

"Did we wake them up?" asked Wee.

"No," said Amnandi.

Wee Eight held out a finger, not to poke but to let a very fat slug slide against the soft tip. "What do they *do* during the day? What do they think about?"

"Unina says there are things we want to know that we will never know."

They'd heard her refer to her mother as this during the ride out.

"I'm calling my ma 'Unina' from now on," Wee declared.

"It's a nice word," agreed Nate.

"She said it means mother with extra," said Amis.

"Unina!" called Amnandi. "What do undereaters think about?"

Khumalo looked up from scraping medicinal mosses into a small pouch. "Mayhem and destruction, my sweet."

The group froze again, wondering if this was true.

They decided it was true, and likely why slugs lived quiet, slow lives.

Restraint.

Amis lowered the log, signal for all to disperse again.

Nate and Wee remained with her.

Khumalo gestured Amnandi to her side and spoke in the language of home. It was nothing of particular importance or secrecy, more a matter of buttressing. Amnandi, though comporting herself well, wasn't generally accustomed to such a group around her. The expenditure of energy was certainly high.

She said to her, "I love you more each day. This is what infinity means."

"The world isn't infinite yet," said Amnandi.

"We'll make it so." Khumalo then nodded at Amnandi to send her off.

As her colorful daughter rejoined the group, Khumalo heard the sullen, noncommunicative one mention to Amnandi, "I like your language. You sound like music. Good music." And because quiet recognized quiet, he left her to her explorations, and himself to his.

His name, from Unina's initial roll call, was Silver.

Unruly Nate: Nate.

Loud Child: Mercy.

Wee: Ahn Wuhn.

Names, Amnandi thought. *Names became people*. If people were wanted. She wasn't entirely sure she did. But it was good to see Bettany showing others how to make an actual usable container out of twigs, and Gita clearly comfortable explaining how a magnifying glass worked.

Even Amis was showing the kids something they'd not seen a thousand times before: how to find the wonder under things that was there all along.

Another reason Amnandi didn't enjoy visiting the village proper was that Waterfall was generally quite boring.

Yet, if there were four more in Waterfall seeking joy, it was enough.

As morning stretched into afternoon with more extensive wandering, Mother Khumalo—content to wander, observe, and teach without teaching—found herself with added shadows. Whenever she studied a root or tapped the ground in such a way as to make a rabbit come out of its warren without running away, Nate and Ahn Wuhn were there, peering, quiet, but questioning when necessary.

Khumalo found their curiosity refreshing. These children, all eight of them, her own included, did not pretend to want to know things; they genuinely wanted to know.

They wanted *their* world.

And would not now be getting this part of it if not for Amnandi, and if not for Amnandi finding good friends, and had those friends not been expansive and charitable.

The nagging question that rested quietly within Khumalo's mind like the undereaters now reclaiming their routines under Amis's log got its answer as Khumalo enjoyed the sun on her neck, the cooler forest wind amongst her scarves, and the look on Nate's face studying the parts of a mantis that might be duplicated in a machine, one he mentally designed on the spot and described in detail.

Amnandi had an outstanding life.

Khumalo's job, then, as mother: maintain that.

Maintenance was something that Ayanda Khumalo, beyond a doubt, knew to do.

By the time eight young bodies mounted their small beasts and made their tired but happy ways home, Khumalo found herself accepting the level of trust the village had placed in her, non-binding yet acceptable.

But would she find that same level of trust, her to them?

It would be a small thing for her to stay there and coincidentally keep her eyes open, particularly as they were never closed, but when was a small thing ever a small thing?

PART TWO

POTENTIALITIES

Constable Bethune knew one unshakeable truth about investigations: things ran toward the inevitable whether investigated or not. The stupid tripped themselves, the guilty bragged, and the malevolent invariably made a bonfire of themselves to ensure their acts be adored, for fewer things lived on longer in the minds of citizenry than a good crime.

But Dotrig, via the village council, which—as any who knew knew—was effectively via Dotrig herself, in sending a foreigner with questions his way, tipped things toward finding out a Thief Mage's acquaintances. Toward gathering intelligence. Even toward corroborating multiple stories, which meant *people*.

"Not an insult," she had said.

True, not an insult. *The* insult. Bethune did his job the way it felt necessary to do so. There was no order in people, and very little truth. The job was to let truth become the virus that it was to most malefactors and let it run its course, bringing them to him as though he were an infirmary.

This, of course, didn't apply to the randomly petty or those so disappointed with their lives, they became violent. Them he found easily enough.

The traveling witch may not have brought magic upon them, but she'd solidified it in his gut.

Magic was hell on the stomach.

His rumbled now and then ever since that looming rainbow had left him sitting at his desk, wondering what in three hells had just happened.

He patted his belly. It was soft but kept memories of lifting and chopping not far beneath. His face had lost most of its tan, but that was because he spent so much time indoors. People had never been his strongest pleasure, and he honestly forgot why he had taken this job. Likely money; it paid well. And the office shack, while small, was nice. He didn't even have to hear the incarcerated, as they were kept in a separate building.

The old man. Stepple. Bethune was aware of Stepple Grandine. Not as anyone important but someone mentioned by various peoples. A masseur when needed, easily forgotten when not.

"And yet," Bethune said to his deputy of precisely one year, Alice Cooney, "he brings news of magicians and plots from an errand boy, himself of no note, and we're to suddenly mount arms."

"Those of no note encounter cracks, sir."

"Perhaps, perhaps, but annoying's annoying, especially in the summer and especially when magic ought best be left to fools and storytellers, of which I am neither."

"What are we to do, sir?"

"Nothing of use. Eyes open, ears open, prepare to meet our gods... Do you know, if nothing comes of this, we're out valuable time and guild money."

"Which will be considered more valuable," she said, meaning the money.

Bethune nodded. "Sharp mind."

"So...we should hope something comes of this?"

The constable picked up his cap of authority and clapped it on his shaggy hair. It was too hot to be out with a cap on. "I am now to meet with this Madam and one of our esteemed populace for no reason whatsoever besides said Madam wanting to assess me like some child. I'd spit, except I'm not outdoors yet."

"Appreciate your waiting, sir."

He accepted Cooney's manners. Manners kept the outside people outside.

"Will Miss Dotrig be there, sir?"

He knew that hopeful romantic tone. *Good luck with that*, he thought. He had his hand on the door. "I certainly hope not."

***

The old man clearly didn't like this. Felt like he was on the path to becoming official, and that wouldn't do. But he kept his patience and tried his best not to eye the constable any more than could be helped.

"I'll be concise," said Khumalo, who had a meeting with Bog at Nowhere before he left. "I wanted both of you aware of important things. The thief, being afraid of me, will not have sent for aid in which he has no confidence. For such as him, confidence means dangerous and powerful, something I sense he was at one time."

"All I saw of him was an old man," said Bethune, "one with the occasional potion and odd insight."

"He is quite old, and I should have heeded that when encountering him, but I was negligent."

"From what I judge of your account besting him, I'd say arrogant," said Constable Bethune.

This drew a glare from Stepple and an assenting nod from Khumalo.

"That one of those 'first time for everything' occurrences for you, Madam?" Bethune continued.

"I will be in your debt if I repeat it."

This brought Bethune up short. He hadn't expected that.

"So, we know where he is, then?" said the constable.

"No," said Stepple.

"I thought you got word from a boy."

"A boy paid well enough to protect his deliveries"—*(as some are unsavory)*—"same for the vendor"—*(she as unsavory as a shank sunning itself)*—"nor can I be paid well enough to illume you as to their persons," said Stepple.

"This is official business," Bethune stated.

"Mr. Grandine and I," said Khumalo, "will confer later. No one in Waterfall is to know of his involvement."

"I'd say that's already pretty much spoilt," said Bethune.

Perhaps it would be, had Khumalo not portaled herself and Stepple to this location of abandoned stalls just beyond Nowhere. As for the constable's presence, people were used to seeing him wander here and there when he wasn't shut up in his office.

They sat on the ground out of sight without ever having been on the mind, behind two shanties that stood solely by leaning against each other.

Khumalo answered Bethune with "It is not" but promised it to Stepple with those three words. "And there's always a possibility of information flowing both ways. I will not endanger my friend. I've done some research in your forests. Trees and roots keep records, particularly of destructive energies. Word of ugly passage has come to them from their mountain kin. Whatever is coming here will not leave if simply asked. And there's nowhere for your citizenry to go."

"Where does that leave us in your stew of hypotheticals?" asked Bethune.

"Me between them and Waterfall," said Khumalo.

Bethune and Stepple had heard enough weariness in their lives to not miss it in Khumalo's voice, though she tried to keep it away.

"And a majority of my hypotheticals, sir," she continued, "would kill you as fact. Your spirit would have no time to prepare."

"Are you sour because you haven't seen what she can do?" said Stepple.

"All I've—"

Khumalo was on her feet so quickly, both men swore they saw an afterimage of her still seated. She threw a portal, yanked Bethune to his feet into it, and left Stepple rooted to the spot.

She emerged inside the constabulary. Deputy Cooney gawked. Bethune gasped. Khumalo threw another portal, pulled Bethune mid-gasp, and vanished with him.

In: along the easternmost tip of the wharf.

In: beside a cave she had found while Amnandi had sailed, in case a place of safety became needed.

In: a desolate hard-packed road, one of the smaller ones leading south toward Suod Province.

She waited for the completion of that one single breath he'd been trying to take.

"This is where I allowed him to encounter me, taking him for a fool. He is."

"Even," Bethune huffed, "fools," huff, "carry knives, miss."

"Place your hands on your knees and stand with your back to the sun. Focus on slow breaths."

He did as instructed.

"This was simply a mode of travel," she said.

He descended from stooping to lowering himself gingerly to the ground, one arm over a knee, the other propping him up, head hanging and eyes closed. "Point. Taken."

"I don't enjoy having to make points in this fashion. I dislike having to make the point at all even more. Do we have an understanding?"

"Yes, ma'am." He rolled to a knee to stand. She assisted with a hand under an arm, doing more than half the work of lifting him.

"I would not waste your time were I not formidable," she said. "Nor will I place myself or my child in harm's way."

He started to speak, held up a finger as a wave of nausea hit, waited it out, then, after a shallow exhalation, said, "What do you plan, in that case, because it seems danger is what we're supposed to be looking out for?"

"Only if met head on."

"Madam, if there's another way, I've not learned it."

"Close your eyes."

"Why?"

"We're going back."

***

When she returned, the twofold mandate was given: for Stepple to give shadows a wider berth in any attempt to gather information, and for the constable to etch the name Stepple Grandine to his protective routine. Discreetly.

VOYAGE

"**A**mnandi truly doesn't want to see you leave," Khumalo said to Bog, who completed the sewing of yet another rip in one of only three tunics he owned. She had never known anyone to tear clothing so often.

He left the edge of the hard cot to adjust the shutters to let in more air. The scars on his arms, chest, and back crossed like trails made by under-skin creatures. Facing Khumalo again, he shrugged his tunic on. She had courteously dropped the spindle of thick thread along with its formidable needle back in the small pouch he kept on his person. The pouch also contained bandages, plus now several new poultices courtesy of Ayanda Khumalo's pestle. He placed it into one of two large thigh pockets, one above the other, on the right leg of his tough breeches. His own design and sewing, he'd said. "I call them cargos."

The cargos were now modified. She'd shown him how to

make the sewing/medicinal pocket waterproof as opposed to the -resistant he'd devised.

Both pocket flaps were now sealed. Bog gathered his tooth scrubber and razor from the sill. He studied Ayanda a moment. She trusted him with everything she held precious, and he was indebted to her for that.

"I told Amnandi I'd be back," he said.

"She believed you."

He checked the room one last time, which consisted of him not moving more than his eyes from the spot in which he stood. Khumalo rose from the storage crate to allow him access to it.

From it he pulled: a rolled leather strip of small throwing knives, a hefty pair of boots; a cloak, a folded, oil-treated tarp, empty water sacks of various sizes, a slingshot made of a wood Khumalo didn't recognize, and four daggers. These all went into a larger pack already on the bed. The dark brown cloak would serve as additional saddle cushioning.

"You didn't tell her where you were going?" He hadn't told Khumalo, but she knew precisely where he was going. There was no point attempting to dissuade him.

"Ride with me till we part?" he asked.

"Of course."

He stopped downstairs at the weapons minder, presented the wooden die that had the number of items due him on it, along with the graphite copy of the minder's receipt listing his items.

He and Khumalo waited in silence.

Shortly, the minder's assistant, a muscular goddess of a person missing only one eye, appeared with a large sword snug in its scabbard, and a double-bladed axe that looked capable of cleaving every ounce of water from the air if need be.

She presented both weapons with the respect of an acolyte.

It was good to have the axe in hand again.

***

As far as anyone in their families knew, the merchant ship *Bane*'s master carpenters Sarantain and Grucca were back at sea. Rarely had two loved so much yet remained so near. It had to be a blessing for their captain, the goddess, and the sea itself!

Families often meant well but were leagues from the mark.

As for goddesses, Bog thought as he gazed at an expanse of trees that seemed to have no preference whether he journeyed or not, there was no guarantee the goddess wanted this for him, but when had the prospect of guarantee ever meant anything between them?

The two had seen him riding fully packed out of the village with Khumalo and knew the taciturn posture of someone determined to face displeasure and spit in its eye no matter the outcome. They did not need to know more than that.

As sailors, packing at a moment's notice was commonplace. A fat bundle each and their weapons from the minder, and they were on their way.

After determining which road he'd taken, their fast horses caught up to him quickly. By then, Khumalo had departed.

Not a word was spoken outside of their three pairs of eyes connecting.

Bog reined his magnificent horse northward.

Sarantain's and Grucca's horses followed.

After the first mile, Bog said, "This will be a long journey."

Grucca answered for both. "We know."

***

Seven days. Five if they rode hard, but the horses hadn't

volunteered for this task.

Seven days, then. The first day, absolutely nothing of note. Talk of recipes, favored weapons, and comparisons of various distant lands each had experienced, to pass the time. Breaks for food, drink, and rest while staring at the sweep of the sky to remind themselves of beauty despite their reason for traveling. Pitching camp and eating once more under darkness so speckled with beautiful light that, though they may not enter its embrace, each man understood grace.

"What we hunt," Bog the Unsmiling told them as the fire ate fat from the spitted hare, "we'll know when we see it."

Sarantain grunted assent.

Grucca sighed, wishing all could simply sail in peace. "Will it know us as its hunters?"

"This is witchery stuff attempting to roost," Bog said in the darkness, his eyes visible only by the fire reflected in them.

"Isn't that best left to the madam?" Grucca asked.

"We're here to see it doesn't touch upon her. Or her daughter."

And that was the last it was spoken of.

The fire crackled and popped its own tales and theories as to what, if anything—for the world was vast, even this small part of it—would curse its luck at meeting them.

Bog was fairly certain, however, that once his party crossed a certain point, the hunt would be reversed.

Crossing paths with the thief's avengers would be prove no difficulty.

***

The betrothed accepted his need for silence. It fed the necessary solitude. The party rode in no clear direction save toward the mountains.

Grucca brought his horse alongside Bog's. "Three days' hard travel. We smell so bad, we're attracting swarms. Another stream should do." He patted the neck of his horse. "Even these could do with immersion."

Sarantain came to the other side. "Summer quests are hell's work, yes?" He gave Bog a grin of support.

"I've traveled this wood before," said Bog. "Water by high sun to the west."

"You're well traveled, my friend," said Sarantain. "What brought you here?"

"Sorcerers."

"Sorcerers are ragged and unpredictable. Nasty business."

"Very much so."

"Thus all the fresh wounds and lacerations," Sarantain duly noted.

"Ayanda gave me salves to speed healing."

"Ayanda," said Sarantain, using the familiar to underscore Bog's clear bond with her, "is likely twice as wonderful a person as her daughter, for she's had time to age. Shall we plan another wedding upon completion?"

Bog looked at him, and for the first time during the journey there was more than flint determination in his eyes.

Sadness was there. But also mirth. Acceptance. Gratitude. Loyalty.

"It," Bog answered, "was a marvelous betrothal," and he clearly planned to say no more toward the question.

"You ate enough, I'd expect you to say no less."

"Grucca," said Bog, "what is best about this man?"

Grucca hesitated not. "He cares deeply, fears few, loves beyond measure, cannot tell a proper joke, and holds chins with fingertips while kissing."

"Fingertips," Bog repeated.

"Fingertips," Grucca reiterated.

"Some day," Bog said, "for me, fingertips."

"Well answered, my friend," said Sarantain.

"Does love explain our presence together?" Bog asked.

"No. You stink like an unbathed ham," said Sarantain.

"One fallen in a pit of fish and can't get out," said Grucca.

"We have no love for you. Ride on."

All three kicked their horses toward water and rest.

***

The stream ran clear and swiftly over many rocks. The horses were led in and rubbed down, then allowed to graze or find shade, whichever their liking. They had refilled all water pouches; man and beast had enough for several days if cautious.

Bog dove, grateful for a sensation along his nerves other than aches. It was a large stream, and deep enough at its center for Bog to travel twice his length without touching bottom.

He did so...and saw the eyes of a raven stare back at him.

He kicked to the surface. "Out! Out now!"

Naked Grucca and Sarantain exited quickly.

"Swords?" asked Grucca, already in motion toward them.

"No," said Bog.

The seabird emerged like a bolt, raining water even as it twisted in the air to wring itself off. It was nearly the size of a small child. It landed on the grasses nearby. It assumed the guise of a diminutive woman, each black feather tipped in gold, gills in lieu of bosom slowly opening and closing.

"Which of your souls is forfeit?" this raven woman said, her tone almost that of a minor functionary.

"None here are for thee," said Bog.

"We see nothing!" said Grucca.

Bog saw her clearly. "But you hear her. Mark her passage in the grass."

"My claim was openly marked," she rasped. "Observe the stones."

"There are no stones," said Bog.

The raven looked to and fro. There were no stones. "Sister!" she shouted at the air. "You have removed my stones again!"

"Bog, speak of this," said Sarantain.

"I am marked by beak and talon to see them."

"You killed a northern king," said the shrill, small thing. "His marks upon you still flush red. You glow with death, murderer."

"Will thee allow me safe passage for thy sister's infraction?" said Bog. To Grucca and Sarantain: "There is a searaven laying claim to this water. She stands ten head away from us just off our left hands. She is unarmed and more dangerous for it. How many have thee taken in these woods, sister?"

Grucca and Sarantain knew from his conversation this was not the prey they sought.

"I don't need many." She gave a small, respectful tilt of her tufted head. "I like the old tongue. It reminds me of when we had much fun with you flightless, skinned voles."

"Bargain: any item I own save my horse and my weapons."

"Should I want one boot?"

"Yours."

The bird in woman's form pointed to their various items of clothing wrung out to dry across shrubs. "If I should want your ridiculous underthings?"

Bog spread his arms wide. "At this moment, I have little use for them."

"What if I require your teeth?"

"I do not own them; I am merely the soil they grow in."

Horses were fascinated by searavens, and drew closer.

The raven drew back. The scent of horses was utterly repugnant. They smelled like twelve humans pressed into one.

"Do you accept that your sister has fouled the game?" Bog pressed.

"I do." She sat unceremoniously, loudly squelching grass between ravencheeks as she did so.

No one reacted.

She was pleased.

"May we dress?" Bog asked.

"Speak to me unclothed only. I find your coverings ludicrous. We've left the majority of the wood to you voles. Why must you despoil *all* of it?"

"I did not murder your king."

"The snapping of an old frail neck is murder, Bog of Nasthra. Even the ravens of your lands await your return to justice."

"Are you being tried for an act you truly committed?" Sarantain asked.

"I killed a king of the ravens far to the north in traveling here."

"Only you voles consider time a stretched thing!" She slapped both hands on the grass, fueling her next outburst. "The viewing of a single moon. It was yesterday, it is today, it is now!"

"King Xixx was by no estimation a just king," said Bog gravely.

"But he is dead. And there is price in death. *Thee* owes surfeit."

Sarantain and Grucca kept tight watch on the grass. Both men were swift, and weapons lay close at hand.

"Speak to them, Nasthran, before they become foolish." The air then spoke directly to Grucca and his lover. "Have you never seen a razor in a tornado? The way it flashes at once everywhere but nowhere you can grasp? How one is dead in the air and bled dry before thee hits the ground?"

"Hold," Bog spoke. The sprite and he engaged in a brief standoff, though she remained sitting.

Witchery stuff was damned annoying. How did Khumalo deal with this so coolly on a daily basis?

"I accept your bargain," the wee one said eventually.

"What will you take?"

"Your time. I will follow you and, should I become displeased enough, select one to die." She stood. Her feathers grew more pronounced.

"I reject your terms," said Bog.

"It was not an inquiry." She gave a hop that turned into a great flap, which shot her skyward, at the apex of which she tucked her wings, became a sleek obsidian knife, and plunged into the stream.

"This, my friends, is what I do."

"By the gods, I had a feeling we'd deal with such," said Grucca. "You and the mum riding through town, I knew it for fact. Both of you felt dark and darker still."

Bog hurried to gather his things. "My brother, we have not even approached night."

The raven came to the surface and skittered wildly across it. Grucca and Sarantain saw the surface as if disturbed by the slapping hand of some angry, invisible ghost.

"What's it doing?" asked Grucca.

"Purifying the waters."

With a raven now involved in this affair, things would likely be very cautious.

**

The following morning:

"How in all the waters of Eurola did we manage to find the one with a malevolent sprite?" Sarantain groused as, high overhead, the giant raven circled, seemingly intentionally blotting out the sun as both metaphor and countdown.

"There are no accidents when magick is concerned," said Bog. "I've suffered with it enough times. There's a magnetism to such odd things. Magick attracts magick."

"We're not magical."

"No, but these woods were once likely thick with it, and if once, still. No matter how many centuries. It's been said there will never be a war for primacy between humans and non; they simply have to outlive us."

"What do we have to do to see it?" asked Grucca, head to the sky.

"Nearly die at its hands. They are beautiful but not worth that sacrifice." Bog shaded his eyes and stared upward.

"It must have been like you were killing a child," mused Sarantain offhand, "with them so small." Grucca grunted to shush him. He shushed and let the wind carry the conversation with whatever unspoken language it held.

"She's good fortune to us," said Bog.

"How so?" Grucca took his eyes away from the clouds to hear this explanation of fortune.

"She hasn't attacked and she hasn't left us. She's curious. Up high, she's probably got a scent of what's coming."

"So, she wants to see a fight. The fae are no better than my pub mate," said Sarantain. "What do we do while she's up there, wherever she is?"

"We ride and learn whistling tunes," said Bog, being sure to catch both men's eyes. "Mind."

Grucca nodded immediately. Sarantain, catching on a moment later, said, "Aye."

While Khumalo and Amnandi studied, the three men rode the day, building off tunes Bog initiated. Short, nearly bird-like ditties. At times, Bog glanced skyward and the pitch would change, or to his right, another pitch, left, another change, behind, a higher double trill. Between the changes, a whistled ditty familiar to sailors. No one recalled where the song originated, but sailors the world over shared it in translation.

It is not my death I sail toward, luv; weep you not so for me.

It is life alone I sail for, luv; I sail this sea for thee.

Any riches are as nothing should they not provide us a home, good rest, and a bed.

The sea takes as it will, when it will, who it will; but it has not yet come for me.

Those who'd tried singing that on the ship got a nudge from Bog. Seeing that, Grucca joined with his own nudge, then Sarantain as well. Whistling was fine, but there had been wee, joyous ears aboard for whom a doleful ballad should be years in coming.

Between whistling and watching the woods, Grucca asked bluntly, "Should we know of anything else you've killed?"

"It would be better to ride."

***

Later, with Mother Khumalo walking Waterfall, casting various protection spells, Amis rode the high noon sun straight to Amnandi's house. She did so with contradictions.

She hated Waterfall, she hated Da, hated fowl, hated everything that ever happened in her life...

...but loved the odd girl who had come into that life, loved that she had been shown impossible things in familiar places, loved the faithful pony beneath her that smelled of Da's liniment for days after a good rubdown.

Loved that her decision to do a simple thing brought her to Amnandi's door.

Amis loved the small home. It looked as if birds had left forest gifts on the roof.

In a cloth bag tied at her waist was a doll carved from wood, adorned with gauzy fabrics in bright colors, and portraying not a smile or coo on its face but a wink. A gift to her from her mother, but Amis was now too old—by her own considered estimation—for such things.

Amnandi opened the door before Amis even had a chance to dismount.

"Don't frown like that without saying good morning," Amis said. She crossed to Amnandi just as Amnandi was about to say, "It's noon," and wordlessly hugged her. At the time when Amnandi would have stepped back, Amis continued the hug, her face tucked into the crook of Amnandi's neck. Amnandi relaxed into it and let the girl receive breaths unhindered.

When Amis broke, she said, "If you can get me close to the mountains, I'll go the rest of the way myself."

"Of course not. Does your father know you're here?"

Amis imagined all the stories her mother could have told her would likely have mentioned it being unwise to lie to witches.

"No."

"Wait here. I will ride home with you."

"Amnandi..." Amis had never considered words extremely useful. There were too many of them, and thus too many to choose correctly all the time. She untied the doll and thrust it forward.

Amnandi studied it in the bright sunlight. Her next words, she wanted to phrase delicately. "Are you aware of symbolic gestures?"

"Even Da is aware of symbolic gestures. He tells me my chores are symbolic gestures. He's not stupid. I'm not stupid."

"You are extremely intelligent."

"And I'm not a child." Amis held up a warning finger. "You know what I mean."

"It would be better if you talked to your Da."

"I don't know how." This brought tears from Amis, but the

determined child ignored them, ignored them as surely as she knew Amnandi ignored them as any factor in her decision-making.

The child was likely to wander the woods alone, likely to the point of getting lost, likely to cause an undue interruption in lives that knew nothing of hers. Unina had already advised not to go beyond a certain point in the woods.

A series of throws, then. She had promised Unina she wouldn't portal with friends, not again in Eurola, but if she and Amis weren't actually going anywhere, and Amis was clearly familiar with the act, and if the aim was to keep harm from a friend determined to seek it, was there danger? It would constitute a lie only if she didn't tell her mother. She decided she would.

Amnandi quickly mentally plotted the course. Take Amis places Amis had never seen (it was guaranteed the scruffy girl had not wandered the woods as much as Amnandi and Unina had). Amis would believe they traveled outward.

And would eventually tire.

One final question would ensure her friend would consider the doubts in her own mind.

"How do you plan to get back?" Amnandi saw Amis's resolve falter. "You see? Nothing we do is us alone. You would need me."

Risks to a nine-year-old mind were varied and great. Needs, however, always outweighed them. "I'll keep you safe," said Amis.

❋

An Unnamed Raven spotted a shape far northward of three riders and considered leading it in their direction but got curious. The raven had inhabited five different streams since encountering a malevolence as single-minded and large as what the beast gave off, a twisted fog of preternatural doings about it, dragoon-like but without charm. The hulking shape didn't so much as move through the forest as the woods, dirt, and rocks parted from it to avoid accidental touch.

It was twice as large as the king killer and foolish bargainer, Bog, and, even as high as the raven circled, lent the wind an air of rot.

The raven knew this thing. A true demon trapped on this barren land, compared to the bounty of its demon realm, was not a thing to forget, never fully. There was always room in memory for nightmares.

A sudden violent current, as if summoned by the raven's unkind, errant thought, slashed the updraft the raven sat astride, throwing the giant bird into a startled wobble.

When she righted, the wind came at her again.

The wind might mistakenly disrespect a searaven once but never twice. The Unnamed Raven closed its eyes to see the unseen, throwing the universe into a swirl of colors, auras, energy matrices, and the revealing of those beings whose very souls bent light.

She saw the tatter that called itself alive intending to collide with her.

She gave a great downbeat flap of wings, blasting her upward as well as releasing a barrage of feathers more lethal than any double-edged blade.

The feathers shredded through the tatter (the raven felt its pain), but the thing still came, twisting itself into an upward-screaming spear straight for the raven's head.

The raven wrenched her body and grabbed at another current, putting just enough space between herself and death that the spear raced harmlessly past. Before this new airborne malevolence could right itself, the raven folded its wings and angled its beak, streaking downward and away so fast, none but another of her kind could hope to catch her. The searaven had felt the presence of this tattered sickness before, too, as it had the hulk. And she remembered its name.

Raggle watched the bird until it was merely a dot skimming the horizon-top of distant trees, then resumed her ragged journey toward her brother. She was not happy with the daylight at all.

On a hill far below, in open land for a change yet himself being only human so of no consequence, Bog lowered the telescopic sight he periodically trained on the raven. The raven had veered off in that direction four times since daybreak, always returning to remind Bog of her omnipresence.

He had his brothers follow him on a change in course.

CHANCE, CHANGE, RAGE

It can be fascinating how things change. The circular plan had worked until places that weren't the same started to seem the same. Amnandi thought of taking her to the burnt ground and telling her it was as far as she could go, but she didn't want to go there herself.

Inside herself, she didn't want to admit to limitations she did not understand. Yes, fatigue was one thing, yet ability quite another. She could *see* the mountains. If the resistance she felt earlier was her own doubt, she had the certainty of a ten-year-old that she could erase it. She could make this one daring trip—alone at first, then quickly with Amis—and afterward practice diligently so that such trips were commonplace. Only then would she show Unina.

No wind, she told herself, *will stop me.*

Nor had it. She stood on a high bluff visible from many of their play-area vantages. More rocky, less green, the air scented more with longing and less of conifers. The instant Amnandi's foot touched the hard ground, she turned to appreciate the expanse of how far she'd come. Very, very far. It felt like an entire world's worth of trees, grass, and sky. Her friend wasn't even visible at the end of that world, but Amnandi knew from where her own bright mind had come. And she knew—casting the energies for the portal spell—

She could get back.

"Well?" said Amis. Her entire small body squeezed the word out.

"It is as far as we go." Amnandi took Amis's hand. "Close your eyes and take deep breaths."

Amis closed her eyes. Inhaled. Felt Amnandi's tug forward. Wanted to exhale but felt any need to breathe had dissolved.

Felt a change in the wind temperature and speed—actual wind—and the ground under her worn soles poking upward rather than the calm of a forest bed.

She opened her eyes.

She exhaled.

The Great Crescent Range's snowcaps greeted her so much closer than they ever had before. They were practically kin.

Not practically.

My sister, Amis thought, and didn't care that she immediately cried. "Can we go farther?"

"No. My entire mind says it is not safe, and I have learned to listen to them. You should learn it too," said Amnandi. "Plus, my head hurts."

The sporadic white tips gave way to shades of gray, which in turn became splotches of brown and green gaining in prevalence as the mountain slid into its gradual commingling with the land below. Even with an entire forest between the bluff they stood on and the mountain proper, the entire weight of the range sat on Amis's mind. The serrated tops, more than merely teeth, were *her* teeth. And her mother's. Especially her mother's.

"This is good," Amis said, sitting. "Are you fine?" But her attention was on untying the cloth bag containing the doll and other items: a cube of hard cheese, a small, stoppered bottle of ink, and a blue feather. "I brought the feather just to show Ma and the mountains; I'm not going to leave it." Amis regarded Amnandi, who was also sitting but with a frown below her colorful headscarf, with closed eyes, with rigid jaw.

"Nandi?"

"Perform your ceremony."

"I don't know that I have one. I want to place this high in a tree." Amis smoothed the woodcut doll's crumpled linens. "Da says Ma wrote stories."

Amnandi gingerly opened her eyes, shielding them to search out the best tree. A stout one in easy walking distance with thick branches called to them. Amnandi started off. Amis repacked her treasures and followed. Her friend walked with the resoluteness of someone in pain, and that worried her.

At the tree, as both looked at the great green of it, Amnandi asked, "What was your mother's name?"

"Savannah."

"We do this for Savannah," Amnandi told the tree, accepting its silence as permission. She threw a portal, brought Amis in, and with the next step, both stood on a wide, high branch.

Amis placed the doll and cheese at the crook of trunk and branch. She left the ink in the sack, stuck the feather behind her ear amidst her hair, took a bite of the cheese, then dropped it back in with the ink, and used the strip of cloth around her narrow waist to tie both bundle and doll to the branch.

She turned just as her friend's eyes fluttered closed, her sandaled feet slid from the limb, and her butterfly body tipped toward nothing.

"Nandi!"

The scream snapped Amnandi's eyes open. Amnandi threw a portal, fell into it, and fell out in a tumble on the unyielding ground.

Amis waited moments to see when Amnandi might catch her breath, regain her composure, and glance upward with that sigh of an old woman Amnandi had learned so well.

She waited.

Amnandi did neither.

Of the two children, it could be said that Khumalo found them quick, except that she did not.

If not for something prowling the daylit sky.

Raggle found them quicker.

***

"Is my niece here?" Tourmaline asked the moment Khumalo's door opened, the sun on the wane.

"No."

"You let your daughter go all day?"

"The children are often in the woods the better part of the day. Their duties are still light in the village."

"My brother saw Amis at breakfast, left her to her chores while he tended matters at the port. Returned home, she wasn't there. Waited two hours, she wasn't there. Rode in to check with me—she sometimes shadows me at work. He's out now gathering searchers. Bettany and Gita have been home all day. The village has been prepared to be wary. What can you do to allay my fears?"

"Wait here." Khumalo threw a portal a half-step after walking past Tourmaline's green skirts.

She exited at the children's favorite spot in the woods. A deer regarded her and the hole in the world quizzically.

The next: a stream.

The next: deeper spots in the woods, each time immediately casting for a sense of her daughter's mind.

The docks: nothing.

Four more successive portals.

She returned home.

Tourmaline's agitation was palpable now.

"Wait here," Khumalo said. She entered the home.

Tourmaline called out into the quiet dwelling, "What are you doing?"

"Gathering needed things." Khumalo exited carrying nothing. "I have what I need," she said to Tourmaline's silent query. "I will return successful. Trust that." She threw the portal. Tourmaline walked straight toward it, stopping inches from its electric edges to regard Khumalo.

"Trust this," said Tourmaline Dotrig, waiting with no intention of staying behind.

Khumalo entered and brought her along.

***

The unmistakable tang of strong magick drew Raggle down from the skies.

The exquisite aroma of fear brought her to the branch with the child, and it was so easy to put children to sleep to feed.

The small one hung over the limb like a forgotten rag.

Raggle settled over her.

The taste was sharp. She felt the little heartbeat increase as though chattering, as though suddenly very, very cold. She billowed and flared around the child—a snack, really—but quickly turned her attention to the one on the ground. That one emanated magick in overlapping waves.

She would not drain them entirely. The trip to Twitswaddle took considerable energy, and even now, there were things interfering. Wretched ravens seeing her when she did not wish to be seen. Living off the fear of animals had made Raggle stingy with real meals. Perhaps she would rest there a bit, let the nutrients of children's dreams populate her veins and nerve endings slowly. Give Bash time to catch up to her. She'd even save Bash the snack bones.

Nothing is wasted, she thought proudly.

Her talons had firm grip of the child. Just a bit more from this one.

The one on the ground would be next.

***

Khumalo, meditating on the grasses, opened her eyes to a sight of Tourmaline Dotrig pacing, who still thought meditation ill-advised at this time despite the witchery and magick it likely entailed.

Khumalo, Tourmaline noted, looked far from accepting or enlightened.

"The veils were emptied," said the sharp-faced woman.

"I know you don't expect me to know what that means, but—"

"Do not interrupt. My daughter exists differently than myself. I've traveled to each of her comfort universes. Silence."

"You haven't left here."

"I had hoped Amnandi herself could assist me in finding her."

Khumalo rose slowly, her mind still attempting to coalesce. She and Dotrig had traveled to many places. To Dotrig's credit, the pale woman hadn't exhibited nausea or vertigo once. Even now, she stood ready.

As an administrator, Dotrig was unafraid of being blunt. "Is she... Are they... Is she dead?"

"No."

"Why?"

"Because I forbade it."

***

Raggle had never encountered a barred way before. Unseen to her, in Amnandi's mind, eight hands pushed back against the ghost. No crack to seep into, no wafer of a gap to slide under. Raggle's talons held firm to the child, but the child may as well have been stone. Yet Raggle sensed the meal would be great, that perhaps a measure of patience would present a tender, unprotected spot, so the gray ghost settled her tatters onto Amnandi, completely enveloping the child, to wait.

***

High above the ground in a tree, the searaven peeled the fur from a bear cub and snipped choice pieces of flesh, snapping them up with a *clack clack* to slide down her gullet. Ravens loved dinner but had no concept of theater (though they loved spectacle). The Unnamed Raven loved the show below. Three people searching the great wood, obviously ready to kill. Shadow beings like herself all having tucked away as they caught hint of powerful, terrible magick to come. Magick in a way that hadn't been felt in far too long. Urges. Even some of the animals hid. Magick may have been gone for a time, but a dangerous storm after a dry spell was still a dangerous storm.

There were few greater spectacles than powerful beings at odds.

She could be seen by those not marked by beak or talon if she wanted them to see. As she snapped up piece after piece of cub, with Bog and the other two brutish ones unaware of her watchful eyes, she preferred *not*. The brutish humans traveled as though destiny wrote itself in sync with each horse's hoofbeat, and that nearly guaranteed death, disappointment, various heartaches, and possibly, very likely for dessert, betrayal.

Writing down these events would introduce a new variable into Raven culture, and she was all for new things. Humans were forever going on about books. New things shook up boredom. But doing so now would interfere with her meat. She preferred her meat.

Besides which, when all was said and done and the great heartaches, betrayals, small battles, and large wars were things of the past, she could relive them through the trees' records. Trees always kept record.

***

Far below and many steps away, Bog, Sarantain and Grucca halted. Bog, touched a hundred ways by a hundred different magicks, be it raven, spell, curse, lightning, or a sorcerer's breath made poison, found himself sensitive to its sibilant stirrings, not always and never understood as more than unease making its intentions known. The intentions usually announced dread, an enclosing sense of something inevitable beyond any experience that made him Bog of Nasthra.

He paused now to let it have its say. He looked nowhere and

everywhere, and that was enough for Grucca and Sarantain. They drew their crossbows, one's eyes high, one's eyes low.

They all listened, but the woods kept on as though nothing important occurred within its bounds that day.

The forest did as it did.

The wind was the wind.

Dry leaves remained dry leaves.

The scents of pine, loam, dirt, and fecund grass divulged not a single hint of everything the natural world knew beyond mortals.

Bark appeared as bark.

Bog faced the two. "I had a sense of anguish. A sense of fire."

Grucca's nose was better than Sarantain's, but in open forest, even a broken nose knew the scent of smoke. "I smell nothing."

"Witchery stuff?" Sarantain put to Bog.

"We swim in it. From this point forward, trust no shadow lest you cast it yourself."

When, after riding quite a bit more, the group passed the tree in which the Unnamed Raven continued to dine, Bog whistled the shanty, hitting notes that were especially high.

AMNANDI

They wouldn't let her dream. Green, Blue, Black, and Red. She desperately wanted to. Felt she *needed* to, that health waited there. The sharp pain cracking open her forehead would go away with a single dream.

They surrounded her. She was low, on a colorless ground, hugging her knees, their colorful backs to her, their eyes guarding outward. As much as she wanted to dream, she had learned to be quiet when they protected her. It didn't happen often, and never without good reason.

Yet she was aware she was shivering. It was cold, very cold, freezing her blood at the source: her heart. It was difficult to breathe with lungs of ice. Amnandi Green, Amnandi Blue, Amnandi Black, and Amnandi Red kept pockets of blood unfrozen, brought air to her in pinpricks, kept calming silence all around her.

And very, very diligently prevented any dreams, leaving only *her.*

She abided despite the cold.

She hoped their trust in her resolve was not misplaced.

She wondered why she felt like she was being suffocated beneath rags.

She also wondered why she felt like she was being slowly eaten from within, as if an undereater had come upon her and found her sweet indeed.

What she knew, however, was that the only way she would give in to the bite was if she were dead.

***

If it was possible to get to know someone intimately in five minutes, Dotrig did so. She knew the tight set of Khumalo's jaw when confounded. The chew of the left cheek when stumped. The eyes that could set fire when annoyed.

The calm that reminded that fury didn't always announce itself. A tone of voice that said there was no alternative to anything it said but to comply.

"Turn away," said Mother Khumalo. "What I do now is not for you to see. Remain that way until I return."

Tourmaline turned away.

Khumalo stepped out of her sandals and reached into the pocket dimension within her robes. She withdrew a mask, its wood smoothed by countless hands before her, etched with whorls and sigils that drew the wearer's soul in line with the mask, each marking looking as new as when a chisel first danced with the flesh of an honored tree. It was a rich, simple wood, lightweight despite being aged nearly to petrification. Stained with such precision that not a drop leaked into a single etching, leaving the lighter markings the appearance of glowing.

There were no eyeholes.

Khumalo slipped its canine features on, caught scent within the mask of her own soul, her daughter's energies, and of another.

She became the hunter.

Claws grabbed hold of the earth, and, with a running push so swift and strong, Tourmaline felt the air pull away, the woman called Mother Khumalo was gone.

Raggle sensed the raven circling but she refused to leave the possibility of this meal. The child would falter. Children always did. This meal would be air rushing into a musty cell. Nectar after solely mud. The potential in the child was staggering, daunting even, that last being another reason to keep her shrouded and asleep, if nothing else. The last time Raggle had felt daunted was when the humans wielded powerful sorcery and ran her out. Perhaps Bash would actually manage to lumber her way; she had tried to keep him somewhat tethered to her locations, but the old connections were worn. He might easily shrug it off as indecision on where he should be.

She considered draining the tree-trapped girl entirely, but if this small, tough one didn't crack, there was always time for that one.

There was also a chance of Bash arriving to hurl a boulder at the annoying raven, clipping its wings. Raggle had never had a searaven.

It would be good to slurp its cawing dreams.

***

The thing at times looked made of smoke, at times a cancer of wet detritus that pulsed. It covered Amnandi except for a foot and hem of orange robe. Bog spotted it from a tree, having to immediately refrain from leaping down with axe in hand.

Instead, in his mind, he did calculations on wind and distance, on angles and vantages.

He climbed down, shared the results of these calculations with Grucca and Sarantain, and sent them on their ways.

Through long lenses, the men sighted each other's signals and moved accordingly along tree branches. All three were expert sailors and had been on enough riggings and masts for quiet, sure footing. Not so much as a limb creaked or leaf fell.

It took the better part of two hours for each avenger to find spots which gave Sarantain and Grucca clear lines of fire from maximum lethal distance away, and for Bog to be within swinging distance of the child in the tree.

Another twenty minutes to watch the thing occasionally shudder as if expending great effort.

Bog found it difficult not thinking for this eternity, but not impossible, not with the assistance of the battered axe's weight upon his back. He had asked the smithy to include minerals in the steel so the axe would always appear covered in streaks of dried blood. The axe helped him be a beast in waiting.

If the thing below fed—and, like the nightmare tick it was, it clearly did—it could bleed.

If either child were injured or worse, the thing would give its blood to the dirt until the dirt ran like slurry.

Bog didn't look at Amnandi's foot or the limp child across and below from him, only the thing, letting its patterns of behavior adhere to his subconscious. It was still as a stone for minutes after each wrenching shudder.

He bided his time.

Quietly, he jumped upward to give himself sufficient velocity, swung past the tree between himself and the one with the child, swung his axe into the trunk of the child's tree to stop himself, and hugged the rough bark, one foot around solidly on the tree limb, nearly brushing the girl's hair.

The thing lifted immediately. Grucca and Sarantain released. Slender, short arrows whispered toward the only physical targets visible: wide gray hands veiny as twisted roots. Grucca's found its mark, burying itself in a palm. Sarantain missed, reloaded amid its howls, and let fly an arrow straight for the wraith's midpoint, where it found purchase and a shriek so loud, it pained them to hear.

Bog snatched up the child, pushed hard from the limb, and swung to the midpoint tree, where a rope was slung to allow him to rappel downward, slowed only slightly by having to do it one-handed.

The bowmen released two more shots. The arrows passed through without effect.

"It makes itself a ghost!" said Grucca.

The thing didn't seem to know what to do: attack its attackers or feed.

It quickly shuffled back to the fallen child, stopping short of touching her head but allowing a tatter ending in a dagger point to hover directly over it.

***

Raggle would see how long these damned humans would wait. How long till they crept closer. Which would be the first for her quick, sudden talons to disembowel.

Bog raced to the scene, axe and sword in hands, stopping several paces away. Sarantain and Grucca swiftly rappelled to join him, trapping the thing in a wide triangle, their bows trained on its dark, roiling mass.

Above, a circling raven.

Bog took note of the ichor slowly leaking from the thing's wounded hand. "Speak in whatever tongue you own."

"This meal is mine!" came the angry rasp. The dagger of smoke above Amnandi's head was replaced with an uninjured hand, its talons poised for the soft parts. "Is your arrow faster than my—"

Grucca shot. The arrow went straight through the flesh between thumb and forefinger, lodging in the tree behind.

"It is," said Grucca.

Raggle spun away from Amnandi and went straight for Grucca. She knew now the sound of the *click* preceding the release of a bow and, hearing it at her side from Sarantain, went immaterial until reaching Grucca. She slashed out before ramming him, hoping for his throat or eyes, connecting only with the crossbow quickly raised in a block.

The bowstring severed. The big man brought the crossbow's stout wood down in a strike that would have snapped the neck of anything that had a neck in one place, but this thing was an assemblage of bones in motion.

Yet he struck something and the thing howled again. Howled before raking his face with one sharp tip while slashing him across the thigh with the arrowhead in the other.

Sarantain was closest to Amnandi. He snatched the unconscious child from the ground and raced her to Bog, who in turn raced her toward his horse set back in the woods. He laid her beside the other across his saddle.

Or would have had the wraith not closed the distance so quickly, it speared him in the back. Not pierced but affixed. He felt it against his spine. It attempted to envelop both him and Amnandi. It attempted to seep into his eyes. He closed them. It attempted to seep into his brain, entering his ears, pressing his thoughts.

Suddenly, the thing knew this was both mistake and a boon.

The human did something nothing had ever done before in

Raggle's ancient years. He grabbed back, his mind not repulsed but snatching her toward him despite the fire with which her spirit burned. She tried to recoil, for lesser beings were not meant to see the face of Raggle, then she immediately reminded all that she was the hunter, she was the dream with its throat slashed, the nightmare unending.

The injured hand was slow to smoke, as was her midsection. The hand was yanked hard and back by someone unseen, for long moments stretching her outward like a tendon about to snap. Hands swam frantically through her, grasping at anything still physical, pulling bits of her out of place.

She whirled upon this set of hands, a mouth flashing knives, long oily hair obscuring all else.

Then, when she was pulled far enough from the two bodies she hoped to trap, the thrust of a good blade from inside her umbrella, one so sharp she felt its coming and going as separate lightning strikes.

At this, the tatters congealed into a brief storm of physical pain...then collapsed.

Smoke rose from the ground where, at Bog's feet, ichor quickly pooled.

At Bog's leg, just above his boot, five gnarled, pointed nails plunged into his flesh, turning the thing's gray hand rust red.

"Before I am struck," it gurgled, away from Bog's sword and toward Sarantain and Grucca, "I will pour all the poison my soul can summon into him."

Sarantain looked to Grucca. Grucca looked to Bog.

"Take her. Be swift," said Bog.

Sarantain grabbed Amnandi and ran.

"Go as well, friend," Bog said to Grucca. "Ensure her safety."

Grucca glanced at the skin of evil, a ring of dead grass already surrounding it.

"It's near its end," said Bog.

Grucca stared him dead in the eye. "Will you be standing when I return?"

"I promise it."

***

Grucca and Sarantain traveled two miles southward, sleeping charges draped over saddles, when they realized they were being hunted. A blur at a distance, not quite revealing itself but not hiding either.

Studying.

They stopped. Dismounted. The tourniquet around Grucca's thigh wound glistened. He ignored all discomfort. They tied their horses to trees. Removed swords from their back scabbards. This hunter was too swift for bow. This would be a close-range battle.

They moved a good distance away from the children while keeping them in view.

The woods were preternaturally quiet, as if actively aiding the hunter. Each man's steps, though whispers and sure, sounded to them kin to dry leaves and kindling.

"I much prefer the water," murmured Grucca.

"Agreed," said Sarantain.

The blur allowed itself to be seen moving closer. Then gone. Then closer still.

Grucca had had enough of eldritch things. "You toy with us toward your own peril!"

It rustled ahead of them, nearer to the children.

Bedamned trees, thought Grucca.

Bedamned bushes, thought Sarantain.

It was circling them.

"Pass to whatever realm or enchanted log you belong to!"

shouted Grucca.

"Be...at...ease," came a voice as if through misshapen lungs and unused tongue. "Are they...well?"

"Speak more," Sarantain directed toward the voice. Something in its tone settled him.

"Am...nan—"

In a flash, Grucca and Sarantain knew this to be witchery, and there was but one who currently ruled that. "Madam!" said Grucca.

"An...swer." It was the voice of a wolf, a hyena, and a mastiff cornering a bear.

"We are unsure. They breathe," said Sarantain.

Khumalo, still hidden from them, pulled off the mask, tendrils of spirit attached to her face from the wood releasing and dissipating.

Her skin hadn't yet returned fully human. Snout and canines slowly receded. Sigils and whorls that had imprinted upon her cheeks in glowing blue fire faded.

Her voice, though gutturally tinged, approached. "Look away as I examine them."

They caught sight of her colors emerging from the thicket. The always-pristine robes were torn in places, snagged in others, and her entire left sleeve was missing. As was her headscarf. They had never seen her without her headscarf. Her hair, like her daughter's, was knotted in rows like military bearers, precise yet artful. Commanding.

Her face frightened them. The anger first, then the skin itself. It moved. Blue lines slowly curled and shifted as though separate living beings themselves. They looked away out of respect.

She examined Amis first, as that would take the least amount of time. Finding nothing immediately dire, she moved to Amnandi, laying her forehead against her daughter's, feeding her reassurance and strength, until she felt Amnandi's guards drop and all parts of her infinite soul rushed together and outward in a great, blind, mental hug.

Khumalo flowed with Amnandi, sent a query of Bog to her, and drew back.

Khumalo replaced the mask. "Due...north?" she said to confirm with the two bedraggled men.

"Due north," said Sarantain.

The woods swallowed all sound, and she was gone.

***

By Bog's estimation, only minutes had passed, but he couldn't be sure. He thought he still stood, but he was on the ground. Asleep. Encoiled by the goddess, her golden scales eternally warm from millennia among the stars, speaking comforts to him. Asking him to dream. Asking him to become a wound, an infected, suppurating thing; wanting to wriggle into that wound like a maggot, not the bright goddess, and never once asking him to speak her name, which was their usual greeting.

Morca.

That thought felt less like speaking her name than calling out to her, and one called out when in danger, in need, or lost.

He realized when he felt the presence of Ayanda Khumalo beside his soul that he was all three things. No words were exchanged, but the soul-meanings were clear.

You are ensorcelled. I have momentarily hidden my inner self from the thing, but it will not last. It is leeching life away from you; do you understand?

I'm asked to dream.

It feeds from your dreams.

I have no dreams to give it.

It wants the pain of your nightmares.

Then it should be careful with its needs.

Bog released all psychic inhibitions in a single, flooding rush.

Raggle saw the wrathful eyes of the goddess Morca;

Saw Bog with his hands inside a giant's back, straining to snap the spine;

Saw children burned to ash under a Raven King's ire upon their unwitting trespass;

Felt the thousand blows to her mind, a thousand sword slashes across the length of her body, the break of countless bones and the deaths of countless hopes...

A life of a man who had deemed himself a barbarian...

All these things should have been food for her. *Would* have been, had he not overflowed her pot and caused a gluttonous fire.

Had he not fed upon the feeder.

She writhed free of him as if a dragoon itself spat at her.

In that moment, Raggle saw Khumalo bent low toward the meal.

In that moment, Ayanda Khumalo's eyes snapped open, spearing Raggle of the Ill Bed.

It was a moment of war.

Khumalo donned the mask, which ceased as wood in favor of a mixture of tree and flesh. The sharp points of nails appeared instantly, nails which raked out in a flash across Raggle's smoky form quicker than the wraith could get away.

This was the second surprise of Raggle's day. She felt every painful rip of those nails through her incorporeal form, and she shouldn't have!

"I have eaten witches!" Raggle shrieked.

The beast in colorful, tattered garb spoke forcefully. "You will choke before you have tasted my marrow." Then it lunged.

Raggle darted skyward. Weakness dulled her speed.

Khumalo leaped and pulled her to the ground, a miasma of smoke, rags, and bones trying its best to flee. The mask lengthened the claws at Khumalo's fingertips, turning her swiping hands into scythes that found purchase in smoke and flesh, raining shreds that smoldered the grasses for yards around.

Khumalo worked from a single vision, a shared image from Bog's mind of what he had seen the thing do to Amnandi.

A vision of her child's motionless foot protruding from this compost of wants and malice, this thing which had now repeated a word two times under Khumalo's strikes, but which only registered with Khumalo on the third.

"Mercy!"

Amis had appeared as dead as a fruit peel on that tree.

"Mercy!" Raggle squawked.

Amnandi. Amnandi had subconsciously communicated a sense of being so cold, each individual cell felt suffocated.

Khumalo danced around the miasma lest it gain purchase on her, each motion accompanied with a swipe, her claws now blackened as though inked.

"Mercy," she heard again, weakly, but not from the wraith.

Bog had managed to roll to face her eyeless mask. The strength to speak left him, so he simply lolled his head in a clear *No*.

Khumalo dug her nails into Raggle's sides, pinning her to Khumalo's will.

"Show me your name."

A flash of Twitswaddle. A flash of a beast larger than Bog and with a passion for death. A flash of Raggle in her prime, feeding unfettered like a swarm of locusts funneled into one.

A flash of the thing's unshakeable hunger for her daughter.

Khumalo raised a hand for a death blow.

"Ayanda."

With that one whispered word from Bog, Khumalo changed

her intent. A witch had to unlearn to kill. The hand plunged into the thing's darkness, found what might have been the neck, and squeezed with enough might to forge diamonds.

Ayanda leaned close to Raggle's flailing hair. "I will burn your soul to ash should we meet again," she said in the voice of a beast. "If you feed on anything more than sand, I will know and find you. If you and your misbegotten kin do not disappear from Erah itself, I will erase all trace of your existence. Tell the Thief Mage all I have said and proceed at your own folly." She raised to her full height, Raggle's throat still in hand, and flung the wraith skyward with as much force as she could, sending the body crashing-snagging through tree limbs, landing where—at the moment—Khumalo cared not.

Care went elsewhere.

Bog's chest rose and fell in the precise manner of a bellows which eventually stops.

Warm breath from her snout roused his eyes open. The eyeless mask was a comfort; she never needed eyes to see him. He laid a hand against the side of her face.

"I'm ready to return now," he said.

"Buying time with your life is the gambit of fools," she rasped.

Bog nodded assent.

Khumalo threw the portal, picked him up, settled him in her arms gently, and carried him across the threshold.

"My axe is in the tree," he said.

They disappeared.

⁂

Khumalo, exhausted, managed to portal everyone, in shifts, to her home. Grucca assured everyone his wounds were only flesh wounds, so she had Grucca and Sarantain lift the huge rain barrels to fill the tub, then had Tourmaline ride hard to find Amis's father. Grucca and Sarantain, without needing to be told, stood guard, one in front of Khumalo's home, one near the tub behind, Grucca's crossbow restrung, both men's bows cocked in hand. Bog was laid out by the tub.

Khumalo tended the injuries along the girls' ribcages first, five punctures at their sides making them look like gilled creatures. The salve she slathered smelled of tar, oranges, mint, and pine. The girls barely flinched as she applied the medicine bound with magick deep into the talon marks. She stripped them fully and wrapped their torsos in clean scarves—likely the cleanest, brightest clothing Amis had ever worn—before carrying Amis outside. She placed her on the grass beside the tub. The small one's legs looked as though blood had never graced her veins.

Khumalo entered the shack for Amnandi and a pouch of the salve in powder form. She carried her daughter outside.

All this in silence.

The powder gave the surface of the water a mossy green, oily hue. The water heated as Khumalo stirred it with her forearm.

She settled the children into the water, cast a glance at the nearby stone firepit to light it, and asked Sarantain for more wood from a pile of random branches against the shack's rear.

Amnandi's shivering agitated the oily water.

"I will not be able to maintain the fire. Focus and strength are needed here. Do not let it ebb."

Sarantain nodded.

"Can you tend to Mr. Grucca and Bog?" she asked.

"I can. I've thread for sewing as well." He took the salve from her and bandages from his saddle bag.

Even in the water, Amnandi's normally healthy skin looked ashen. Her knotted hair had all the life of spent coals.

After thirty minutes of sweating into the water, turning it a deeper shade of green, Amis was the first to open her eyes. The fear that Khumalo saw in them broke her heart, for it wasn't fear of their terrible experience; it was of Khumalo.

Ayanda kissed Amis on the forehead, then lay her own forehead against the child's, saying nothing, breathing evenly as Amis matched her breath for small breath, until Amis drifted asleep, as dreamless as the witch was able to make her.

Amnandi remained asleep. Her mother's swirling of the water was in specific patterns, sending sustenance through its wave action. Now and then, Khumalo took her wet hand from the water and placed it on Bog's bare chest, letting the beady hairs trap as much moisture as they could. She was grateful for Sarantain's silence when he'd cleaned and wrapped Bog's wounds beside her.

She was grateful, too, that Bog had not muttered about the axe again. He knew enough to sleep.

A good portion of the search party approached just as summer announced evening in the usual purple and golds. Amis's da was a small, squarish man with large fingers that reached out the moment Tourmaline pointed toward Amis, as if he touched her from across that distance or willed himself to her, even the thinking of which was a kind of magick.

Amis opened her eyes.

Sawyer Dotrig took in the sight of the large man lying on the grass, scratched and bedraggled as though he'd lost a fight to Connie, the largest hen on Dotrig Farm; took in the tall, obsidian woman standing over a makeshift tub with not one but two children in it, the second one surely her own; saw another huge man with a crossbow at the ready, and wondered what exactly his daughter had got into. Briefly wondered. The bulk of him rushed to Amis's side, instinctively knowing not to disturb the water.

Khumalo did not interrupt the pattern of her swirl as she spoke.

"They must remain in the water overnight. You are welcome to stay."

And that he did, on a pallet on the grass near the warmth of the tub.

All night, the woman stirred the water.

***

When Sawyer awoke, that woman, the stirrer, was still there. In the light of day he saw that she was dirty, her fine fabrics bramble-ripped, thorn-torn, and—in places—stuck to her in blood.

Amnandi opened her eyes.

Khumalo, like the automatons the toymakers sold, continued to swirl.

The big man who'd been unconscious when Sawyer arrived emerged from the shack with a bowl and a limp. He set the bowl down beside Sawyer, took the woman gently by the shoulders, and led her inside.

He came out not long after with a stool and a very large sword, and gestured for the other large man—who'd taken quick naps through the night and who had not let the flame die down—to take the empty pallet that still bore his indentations.

Sarantain relented. He was as asleep within minutes as his husband, who had tried to keep watch during the night despite his "flesh wounds."

Sawyer Dotrig took up perch by the edge of the tub, allowing his hand to slide into the water and entangle in his daughter's hair.

Bog planted his sword tip in the soil, both hands on the hilt for support, eyes wide open.

Both protectors remained that way, moving only when each heard Amnandi—who had quickly fallen back into her floating sleep—awaken crying.

***

Though it was summer, Amnandi requested more and more wraps. She no longer shivered, but her insides, she said, felt like snow.

Her eyes, her eyes were significantly older.

By then, Bettany, Gita, their parents, and Tourmaline were there, as was Constable Bethune, whom Amnandi didn't know. Each time she acknowledged Bettany and Gita with a silent nod between all three of them, she wanted to cry.

They loved her.

But she knew she and Unina would have to leave again. This was the way.

Khumalo had tried to stay awake when they told her Amnandi had roused, but even for her, there were limits. Looking around, Amnandi felt it was up to her to be the witch of the moment. From the floor where she sat holding her sleeping mother's hand, the small witch gathered the strength to say, "I am sorry for all distress caused. I am sorry for my foolishness. I am..." Her throat constricted, her tears fell, her friends looked on with deep concern. "...sorry Amis was hurt." Here the dam burst. She squeezed Unina's hand so hard, Khumalo awoke and immediately folded her in a hug, speaking words in a language no one else but Bog knew but all understood.

Amnandi quieted. Khumalo waved her two young friends over to them. Bettany and Gita embraced mother and child tightly.

"We have to leave again," Amnandi said, picturing burning homes and charred earth. Feeling the loneliness.

Khumalo felt the held breath in her daughter's friends' bodies, their clear and immediate dismay.

Khumalo shushed her. She kissed her forehead, then both cheeks. "We go nowhere," Unina Khumalo said, her warm overnight breath stale against Amnandi's cheek yet, to Amnandi, soulful, strong. Sweet. Her daughter's huge, wracking sob of relief reverberated through bone and soul.

***

Raggle's tatters, entangled in the branches of a tree like a ravaged paper lantern, lifted with each breeze and settled with their passing. Hawks avoided roosting anywhere near that tree, but the impossibly large raven flew overhead. Raggle knew it laughed at her.

She was too weak to care.

The breeze continued lifting and dropping her.

The raven, bored, left.

The rising sun settled full on Raggle, seeping painfully into cuts, rips, and full-on fissures in her being.

Raggle of the Ill Bed was a goddess! Yet the witch had been thorough.

She painfully disentangled and let the wind carry her off, in case the witch returned. She did not know where she was when she settled.

But it was again in a tree.

Raggle cried. She cried and cried and moaned, three days, three nights. Cried for Bash, the only sibling of use now, to rescue her.

By morning of the fourth day, she heard the crack of slender trees, the crush of bushes, and the snapping crunch of bones between granite teeth.

The tree she was in shook violently, managing only to ensnare her all the more.

The shaking stopped.

A brief pause.

The shaking resumed, then stillness, then a great *thump* nearer to her, as though something had leapt to hold on. Then a massive *crack* as a fist swung, snapping the trunk far below her. Huge branches shook loose. The one she was on tumbled past the snapped trunk, and she saw the face of Bash not seen for a hundred years. The sunken black eyes of a water beast. The face and snout scarred uncounted times over. The gray brow sweeping back to small, laid-back earpoints. And the tilt of the thick neck watching the crashing limb whip the tatters to and fro.

An abrupt stop. An earth-shaking *thump* on the ground beside her. The slow and methodic breaking of branches until hers was extricated, then her view of the world quickly shifting, the sky arcing closer and the ground dropping away, as Bash picked up the large piece of tree holding her, slung it over his shoulder, and carried her away.

FALLOUT IN WATERFALL

It wouldn't be a good meeting. It wouldn't by any stretch be a good meeting. The guilds were barely represented—Khumalo had insisted on that—and the meeting itself was the most public of public. It was in the open air in the huge stalls area, where most of the citizenry had easy access.

Khumalo, standing atop a rain barrel, had said her piece. Warnings. Details. Evidence and predictions. Suggestions. No one dared a word while she spoke, not even Guildsperson Kieran Horne, who had pushed to the head of the crowd.

The moment the tall, resplendently dressed woman said, "Questions?" Tourmaline Dotrig's gut tensed and eyes roved the assembled for the usual annoyances.

Kieran did not disappoint. "Would we be in danger if not for your daughter?"

Khumalo studied him quickly before answering. The hard expression on her face let him know there was to be no rebuttal. "Yes."

At which, before the assembled poor, he was summarily ignored.

Tourmaline, standing beside the barrel, stepped forward. "As we have already set forth, if there are questions, they are to be spoken to our deputies who, if the question merits, will bring you forth. Do"—she pointed toward those already properly in the process of doing so—"line up at one of the six deputy stations fore, mid, and aft. 'Are we doomed?'" she added, "is not an acceptable query. No more so, I'll answer that anyway, than any usually are." She noted several among the crowd who'd moved forward stop and move back.

A woman spoke a question to Deputy Cooney, who nodded and waved her on.

"Those of us with no knowledge or dealings with magic and unseen beasts, can we learn?" Her tone was aggressive, her stance demanding.

"Magick is not a weapon," said Khumalo. "Any wishing it for such are those who should not wield it in the first place."

"At least for defense," the woman implored.

"I can teach you defensive incantations."

"What of other defenses?" the woman pressed.

"I suggest archers and trenches. Trenches are generally useful in delaying the determined."

The woman, not satisfied, scowled away.

From the rear, a voice amplified through a cone. "What of Suod Province and Barrit? Should we notify them? They could help."

"They would wonder how often have you helped them," said

Khumalo, who didn't raise her voice but was heard back to front. "Am I wrong?"

Tourmaline answered her that she was not.

The next question came from a boy of no more than fourteen years and far fewer chin hairs. His voice wavered. "Will we have to go out there?" He pointed toward the woods and the range beyond. "To fight? To fight them? They sent my mother off to fight the war." The voice broke. "She never came back. Da sits at the window, barely speaking to me."

Khumalo looked to Tourmaline. "What war was this?"

"The last skirmish was with Tox eight years ago."

Khumalo looked to the boy. "Skirmish," she repeated, the word extremely disrespectful to the nights this boy must have faced, an affront to each morning he didn't wish to greet.

Mothers fetched a high premium in this place.

"I task you with this, young steward: stay here and bring voice back to your father. There will be no conscription of the young, poor, or foolishly valiant," the witch said for the benefit of the guildspeople undoubtedly present and who, no matter any emergency, were unlikely to send either themselves or their own.

Khumalo, having her fill of loss and the pains loss bartered with the mind, felt for the boy the same she felt for Amis's fear-filled eyes. Sadness. Shame so deep. A connective tissue between the world and herself needing healing. "If there is a need to take up arms, it will only be those who walk behind me through the village gate. Of their own accord and only as far as I'm able to protect them."

Emboldened by Khumalo's calm, Kieran Horne shouted, "There was no witchery till you came!"

"I think this incorrect. I will research more. History is likely to surprise you, yes?"

Tourmaline nodded at Bethune, who nodded at Cooney, who

moved toward Horne, who quickly shuffled deeper into the crowd.

"No further questions," said Tourmaline.

"One more!" shouted an old woman, older even than Orsys. "Will there be more? What do we do when you're gone?"

"Asking questions of the future speaks to your desire for comforts. Right now, I have no comforts. Not that they don't exist; I simply don't carry them with me. Yet. When I do, be assured I will treat them as a bounty. When I am gone, all of you will remain. That, for now, is enough."

It was not the worst meeting, and Tourmaline planned that it stay that way. The tenor of the crowd had already been felt. Repetition would serve no one. "Should there be further information or questions, the council door will be open."

Constable Bethune boomed out, "Disperse!"

The crowd dispersed.

Khumalo hopped down from her barrel, itching to throw the portal that would take her home, but not yet. She wanted more of the crowd gone and also didn't want to be seen leaving that crowd, even to duck behind something and disappear. They'd have magick enough in their faces, she was sure. Today, questions and fears were more than sufficient.

Tourmaline, standing beside her, served to deflect loiterers from broaching the unspoken worries that were clearly on their minds. The presence of the constable on the other side of Khumalo served as well.

Unina Ayanda Khumalo was extremely uncomfortable, and that was a rarity for her. No one would ever know, of course. She stood straight, her scarf and robe flowed around her in dazzling color, and her face belied nothing she did not want it to.

It didn't take long, however, for Constable Bethune to wander off, and with him the deputies, and with the deputies the bulk of the crowd.

Waterfall's daily life was given back to it.

"I wish you to remain as my liaison with your council. I have no wish to speak to them directly. Not yet," said Khumalo.

"Of course, Madam." Tourmaline shook her head at her own words. "That sounds far too formal."

"We are not friends."

"We're more than strangers. Feel free to call me Tourmaline."

The witch considered a moment. It wasn't that she didn't like the pale, freckled woman; it was that friendship was a precious thing. It wasn't lost that the woman was named after a gemstone. Khumalo respected the providences of greater coincidence just as she paid mind to the results of random chance. She knew of beings who traveled Time differently than she, deities that affected the patterns of lives they found intriguing; even knew of plants that exerted influences over those living near them.

It was foolish to be obstinate for no reason.

"Ayanda," said Khumalo.

"Ayanda. And only in private. A question for you, Ayanda, and complete candor, please. Am I too old to be your apprentice?"

This was surprising. Khumalo even drew back a bit to regard her.

What she saw was a cauldron of sincerity and fire, with the added bubble of a willingness to serve.

"You are not too old, but I question your confidence."

"I face down many on a daily basis."

"And of yourself?" Khumalo raised a hand to stay the answer. "I'll let you know when I am ready for you. We'll see if you have magick in your soul...Sorceress Tourmaline of Waterfall."

"I rather like that."

***

Twitswaddle's entire diet consisted of salted meats. In ancient times, he had considered himself handsome, effortlessly vital. He wasn't sure when his body shrank closer to his bones, when the flesh became parchment, or when he approached meals with hunger rather than pleasureful vigor. The name Twitswaddle had not been a shell. Originally *T'ket Wha'dell*—that much he remembered because in every home, hideaway, or pit he inhabited, he scratched that name into a wall.

Immortality was an addiction lowly humans would never truly understand.

Long life brought with it slow healing if one did not consistently replenish what the body needed. Cells became forgetful. Raggle's had long since forgotten their proper arrangements and shifted her body constantly.

He needed a feeding ground, not samplings. The world—unless he changed it—did not seem it would go back to that.

Salted fish. Salted beef. Salted fish again. At times hare. At times fowl. But usually salted fish. Salted beef.

Ever since that witch.

Had he been at the height of his powers, he would have taken her entire life force, not even leaving time for a panicked prayer to her god. While he paced the cave, he promised himself he'd have bound her energies to his and left her parched beyond Bash's ability to squeeze marrow.

The body, minus pure energies, demanded the physical.

He chewed his hard, dry meat, not even sure which he'd grabbed. Evening settled through the gaps in the thatch door covering the large mouth of his cave. Not that it mattered. The cave was always dark and he'd not ventured from it a single day since barely managing to crawl inside after having slunk his way there. In his mind, *slunk* felt appropriate. The witch had bested him. There was no altering that fact. Hubris should have been exhibited carefully. He had gotten careless.

But then, that was what gods did.

And then got punished for.

Provisions had awaited him in the cave. Despite being a god among lessers, he was no fool. He had caves scattered around a huge section of this part of Eurola, not just Waterfall. Over these long years maintaining weakness rather than gathering strength, he'd learned there was wisdom in being prepared to run away. This cave was well hidden, with the added protection of the rumor he'd spread that many such caves in this area had housed plague families long before, and as everyone knew, plague lingered for as long as it was thought of. No one bothered T'ket Wha'dell out there. Even the delivery boy, pegged rightly as someone who would deliver poison through a storm for his own father's meal if a price pleased him, came only by bird summons per arrangement by him and then-newly arrived sage Twitswaddle, deposited the parcel only after seeing his payment scattered in the dirt, and left without a care for who or what was inside.

Twitswaddle could talk to himself to his heart's content about anything and everything crossing his mind.

He knew his sibling castoffs had gotten his message; the carrion birds told him so. It was only his own impatience that made him pace the cave, wasting precious energies which he replaced by biting down on hard meat; an entire reality centered around vengeance pumped inside whatever he used for a heart. Even his lungs, those lungs she had dared fill with her breath, drew musty air inward for the sole purpose that he, Raggle, and Bash might return to Waterfall and show the humans why humanity had learned to fear the night.

He dared not send a bird out again (it was getting more and more difficult to ensorcell them anyway), as Bash had a taste for them, but it seemed at some point during this forever of waiting, his siblings should have been there.

"Caution, powerful one," he said. "Distances are greater than they need to be when in need, yes? They shrink for those who master Time, not beg it." He dropped the length of meat to the dirt. He would find it again. Nothing had ever come in to steal from the great Twitswaddle.

The cave smelled of death and feces. The cave sounded of insanity and desperation. What bear, rat, or wasp had use for that?

But to Twitswaddle, all was glory. Glory delayed its course, but glory no less.

The woman had taken him by surprise. Somehow shielded her full energies with her scarves and wraps.

And had treated him, T'ket Wha'dell, as a nuisance. He had fed on more entire villages than she had taken breaths her entire *life*.

He traced fingers along the cave wall until they came to rough scratches. The desiccated fingers played over the words.

Yes, his name *was* T'ket Wha'dell, from the old tongue still spoken somewhere on this accursed planet. The name was in stone. Permanent. Unchangeable. Bash and Raggle would arrive. The three would heal each other. The woods, being vast, would always call to wanderers, lovers, and fools, the closer one got to the pitiful things humans deemed civilization. The cave was far enough away from Waterfall for occasional hunting of meals either by swift Raggle or fierce Bash. All three would sup enough, rest enough, then decide how much death visited upon a lesser was ever enough.

***

Of a gray morning's summer deluge, they were there.

Twitswaddle stood outside the cave and saw them...and was

sad. They would further delay his vengeance, Raggle by being ravaged, and Bash, Bash having so little mind left, he was useful only as a marionette.

Bash lowered the Raggle-on-a-stick to the pelted ground, then sat heavily in the running muck, Twitswaddle reflected dimly in his great black half-moon eyes unlit during the day. The brute demon waited, empty but for the need for instruction.

Twitswaddle, drenched in the nightrobe fashionable among Waterfall's elite, turned and walked into the cave.

Bash picked up the Raggle stick and followed him inside.

***

Tourmaline had her first magick lesson: floating in briskly bobbing seawaters well away from shipping lanes.

"You must learn that breath is the most important element of all conjuring," said Khumalo from the battered "official business" rowboat, which barely bobbed at all.

"I swim excellently," said Tourmaline, watching the week's passing dark clouds float parallel to her body. Khumalo had advised she enter the water naked, but Tourmaline insisted on a one-piece suit that ballooned so much, it likely hated water. It was her first lesson, after all.

With her arms and legs stretched out, she looked like a four-pointed sausage.

Khumalo made a hand gesture over the water.

Tourmaline sank three inches under as though a weighted plank had dropped over her entire body.

She thrashed, flipped to her stomach, and swam gasping toward the two-strokes-away boat, spitting both briny water and salty words in equal measure.

Khumalo made another gesture.

The water directly around Tourmaline ceased moving with her, and in not moving, neither did Tourmaline. The sea flowed around the obstacle she had now become.

"First you stopped breathing. Now you're breathing too fast. Which mode of breath serves you best?"

"I don't like riddles!" The wet sausage was not happy.

"Neither do I."

"Are we still being watched?" She'd rowed a fair distance from the docks, she'd thought.

"Not by as many," said Khumalo. "Breathing should protect you at all times, especially when you're unaware of just how much it already does protect you. Breath is your first, best, automatic defense against demons, trolls, or myself. Magick is awareness, and you must learn to extend your awareness."

"Magic involves bobbing in the water," said Tourmaline.

"For hours." Khumalo took up the oars. Beedma waited for her on the dock. "I, on the other hand, must check on my daughter. I will return for you. Breath is your protection."

"Sharks don't care whether I'm breathing."

"There's a large octopus below, keeping watch on your behalf. He owes me a favor. We have history." Khumalo rowed away. When she reached the dock, she patted Beedma, asked her to wait patiently, and portaled her still-fatigued self home.

Bog, sitting on a blanket in the day's calm gloom, opened one eye from the meditative therapy Khumalo had prescribed. "Didn't you say you weren't going to do that for a bit?"

"I have a woman in the water and a horse on the wharf."

An addition had been built (courtesy of Sarantain and Grucca's quick hands) beside the shack. Amis's father, Sawyer, emerged from the addition at Khumalo's voice. He had thus far kept to his promise to enter the home only if Khumalo was present. There were certain healing energies not to be disturbed.

"Good morn," he said as he and she nearly lodged in the threshold, entering at the same time.

"Good morning."

He went to Amis, whose heavy sleep was now due to herbal medicines rather than demonic attack. Both Amis and Amnandi were to sleep long and awaken naturally, upon which they were examined, fed, taken outside for direct contact with grass and sky, then allowed to be quiet until the next cup of tea sent them to bed again. Actual beds, not the serviceable pallets Amnandi and her mother were accustomed to. Tourmaline had them brought in: two small, narrow cots, side by side under the open window at the rear of the shack.

"You're sure still no poison or infection," he said, taking his usual position at the foot of the bed where he could gently squeeze the sheeted tent of his daughter's foot. "She's so pale. Anemia?"

"You're pale. There was little blood loss. I found evidence of natural coagulants." Over the past several days, Sawyer had learned many medical terms from this house. "Victims bleeding to death are of no use to the revenant."

"Monster," Sawyer corrected.

"Monster."

"I'd forgotten monsters were with us."

"They are never gone. At best, they may change their ways. At the least, their appetites."

"That one's wounded."

"Badly, if not dead."

"We know what happens with wounded things."

"We'll conjure dangers another time. Check her temperature as I've shown you."

Two small bowls with gauze in them that collected dew each night sat on the windowsill. Sawyer leaned outward, dipped a finger, and held the finger to Amis's forehead. The water tingled his skin.

"She's fine," he said. He re-wet the finger and repeated it with Amnandi. "Same."

"They'll wake soon."

She left him listening to them lightly snore to prepare their morning meal, casting fire into the wee metal stove. She made sure any dwelling she occupied had a cast iron stove with a belly. She liked the bellies. She considered herself particularly lucky when coming across a large one. There, the small would do. The ingredients for the meal were simple but had to be measured precisely and blended in a particular order and time scheme. Food was no less magick despite eating being commonplace.

She prepared enough for the entire encampment and was thankful Sawyer—in the one-room shack—had learned to allow her to prepare in silence. She could tell he was generally a jocular, talkative man. Now he was just talkative.

He did, however, take to heart her lesson on when to remove the large pot from the heat, how long to let it cool, and how much to give each child.

Khumalo checked on Bog.

"Did I thank you for returning my axe?" he said.

"Numerous times. Please tell me you do not have a name for your weapon." He was quiet. She sighed. "The porridge will be ready soon. Eat. You've had enough clouds for one morning."

"And you?"

She pressed his forehead with a long finger. "I still have a woman in the water and a horse on a wharf."

She threw the portal and was gone.

At the dock, she paused. She pulled an apple from her sleeve. Beedma huffed thanks and ate while her companion let her mind rest for a while.

Khumalo ported into the magickally anchored rowboat,

allowing it to settle rocking, and sat to watch the undisturbed woman. Tourmaline was nearly asleep. Like the boat, she hadn't floated outside the bounds agreed upon by Khumalo and the water. Her ruddy blond hair spread out like blanched kelp. Her limbs continued to look like ruffle-tipped sausages in the ridiculous gray garment, but overall, she appeared a peaceful sausage person. Her long wrinkly toes bobbed to the surface now and then. Her bosom rose and fell synchronously with the waves. Her unbothered breathing spoke subtle magicks outward.

Khumalo settled more comfortably on the rowing bench, allowed a hand the pleasure of the sea, and matched her own breathing to the waves to enjoy her wait.

***

Days later, Bog insisted on riding with Khumalo for supplies. While among the stalls, Orsys sidled closer and closer to Khumalo. When elbow to elbow, the quilt of a woman murmured earnestly, "Are we all going to die?"

Khumalo gathered the supplies she'd purchased from the spice stall. She carried a wicker basket for her things this time, and used a few moments arranging it to assess Orsys.

The elder wasn't anxious or afraid. It was much worse. She was resigned.

"Why would you expect that?" Khumalo asked.

"Stepple."

"Saying?"

"Ancients. Monsters."

Bog, carrying large lightweight baskets, looked over Khumalo's shoulder at the woman.

Orsys returned the glance...and held it.

All right, then. He wouldn't look away.

"Wrong things," Orsys said, narrowing her eyes at Bog.

"I have released many wrong things into this world," said Bog. "I, myself, may be a wrong thing released by someone else. Should monsters arrive, by Morca I swear, they will know me as their elder brother."

Orsys frowned at him.

"Angry brother," corrected Khumalo.

"Bad poetry in this one," declared Orsys. "Do not marry him."

"I hadn't planned on that," said Khumalo.

Orsys leaned toward the witch. "Use him for his body and labor, nothing more."

Khumalo nodded, purposely keeping her gaze off Bog.

"If we are all to die, all monsters must die as well." And with that, Orsys ambled off.

"None of your friends like me."

"They love you. This is why they're honest with you. That conversation is more than Orsys usually speaks around others in entire days." She nested her basket atop one of Bog's larger ones. They headed to the next stall and waited their turn, pretending—again—not to notice the nervous stares.

"I like her," said Bog. "Old Stepple as well. They deserve to live out their lives peaceably."

"You, my friend, think everyone should do that but you."

Bog grunted.

"Your voice has left. Are you fatigued?"

"I am not, Ayanda Khumalo. I am...pensive."

Khumalo grunted. The smell of fresh sweetbreads in the stall lightened her mood. The children had regained enough strength for this treat. "Studious," she offered.

"Yes."

"If I were to marry you, you'd become silly with love. We cannot have that, can we?"

"Marriage is a heinous thing. I'd hoped to talk Grucca out of it."

"It is good, then, that you're a brute who carries my packages for me even though he should mind his convalescence."

"The hag clawed me. I don't wake from bed without something clawing me."

"You, a wrong thing."

"I'm serious about that."

"I know."

"I don't know that I've offered the world beauty."

Khumalo presented her certificate of provision to the stallkeeper and indicated her preference. Instead of the one loaf of bread she was entitled to, the keeper—a quick-eyed, quick-smiling youth barely into the last of her growth spurts—presented two.

Khumalo didn't get the chance to decline.

"Thank you," said Bog, massive hand angling both loaves toward the basket.

Khumalo met the young lady's eyes and, rather than touch her forehead to her, smiled.

She and Bog walked away.

"I did not expect that," said Khumalo.

"No more than I expected my bachelorhood writ *confirmed* using the severed leg of a crow."

"It is a strange world, yes?"

"Yes indeed." He breathed deeply, not realizing how much he had needed something this simple: the surrounding people, the hundred varieties of scents, languages, even the wants that brought each random face to rows of stalls set before a salty wharf. A community could be a wonderful thing.

He would never know. He had made a choice. No home. No land.

No fear.

Choice was not always punishment. Sometimes, it merely felt necessary.

After a short while wandering stall to stall, Khumalo told him, "I know where they are."

Ears didn't linger too near the giant or the witch, so he spoke freely. "How?"

"The raven told me. Catrin. Did you kill—"

"I did." He bypassed her knowing the raven by name now. "What do we face?"

"The addition of a hulk. From the raven's descriptions, a demon from another realm."

"Demons are trapped on Erah far too often," he groused. "It can't be by accident."

"We shall unravel that another day."

"A demon, a wraith, and a thief. I came here," he said dourly, "because I wanted to disappear for a bit."

She let a sparkle enter her eyes, a literal sparkle, leading him away from his faraway thoughts. "We are never where we need to be. At least at times, we're where we want to be."

The unhurried crunch of gravel underfoot was pleasant.

"You have a plan for them?"

"Not yet. But while they gain strength, I gain knowledge."

"Then they are as good as dead."

She cocked a brow at him. "My information and your hand?"

"I'm already bloodied. Not a color to wrap your family in."

Mother Khumalo grunted again.

**

Tourmaline told Amis yet again of how the water had become solid around her. "It was like one of those annoying wandering performers finally getting his hands on an invisible box and torturing me." She spied Bog on his massive steed and Khumalo on Beedma. They approached leisurely but with an air that *words* might have been spoken, heavy words.

The girls were well enough that their sleep time had lessened dramatically. Amis liked sitting outside, listening to her aunt's recounts of various interesting bits of life in Waterfall since—as Tourmaline was determined to affirm—there still were.

While Tourmaline recounted, her brother puttered. Tourmaline had walked up to him days past and said, "It would be good if you learned to talk to your daughter," and left it at that.

He was off gathering wood with Sarantain.

"Are you an actual witch now?" asked Amis.

"I'm learning."

Khumalo dismounted. "I taught you nothing and you learned nothing You were given something. Understand the differences."

"I learned hand motions."

"Have you been granted an audience with a water goddess?"

"No," said Tourmaline stonily as Amis watched the exchange.

"Then these 'motions' would do you no good. Assumptions will get you killed."

"May we speak privately?"

"No. I've had an entire ride of speaking privately."

Bog said nothing. He carried the supplies indoors.

Khumalo knelt face-level with Amis. "How do you feel, my sweet?"

"Like running."

"And you, my sweet?" Khumalo said to Amnandi, her small head uncovered, her feet unsandaled.

"Much better, Unina."

"Tomorrow, you teach Amis simple protection spells."

"Can Bettany and Gita learn too?" said Amnandi.

"Yes."

"Who will tell them?" said Amis.

Khumalo stood. "I will."

"Da can go. He's already said he needs to check the coops."

Acceptable.

Gita and Bettany showed up on their ponies the next day ahead of twenty others, both children and adults—mostly adults.

Khumalo's presence in the doorway of the shack stopped their progress.

Before her mother was able to say one of several variations on "Not in several hells," Amnandi said, "I can do this, Unina," edging past her mother in full red-and-yellow headscarf, blue-and-green robe, and sandals cleaned of any trace of the tatter wraith.

"Do not tire yourself."

Khumalo and Tourmaline left, hearing small Amnandi in the clearing behind the house instructing children—and adults somehow unclear on the concept—on the proper way to form attentive lines in order to even begin to learn.

"It is good that the parents want to protect their children," said Tourmaline carefully.

"Yes."

And that was the extent, as they traveled back to the water, of the ride's conversation.

**

At times, it felt to Khumalo as though she had no gods to speak to, not there. Their influence, it traveled with her, but not the gods themselves. Bog may have invoked Morca from time to time, but he knew she existed for him solely in dreams until he returned home.

Tourmaline did well with the breath. It might do her well

should the administrator need to be of use. It would keep her from panicking. The only reason demons, wraiths, and thieves had not overrun the world was because calm minds existed. And would always do so.

Amnandi was safe, Khumalo told herself over and over as the rowboat bobbed slightly.

What could have been did not exist.

Amnandi was safe. Amis was safe.

The wraith had laid claws on her daughter.

Khumalo dived into the water, robes and all. If Dotrig could be a sausage, she could be an angel fish.

She floated on her back beside Dotrig. She breathed along with Dotrig. Tourmaline, entranced, made no note of her.

Both women remained that way for a long time.

In her heart, Khumalo felt like she, wraiths, thieves, and demons raced to see who would gain strength first.

Her body dipped a little lower in the water. She reset her breath and started again. Atop the water, not in, was the goal.

***

"I know I don't know her well—" said Tourmaline to the gathering of herself, her brother, Bog, Sarantain and Grucca.

"We know her least," said Grucca.

"—but she's been snippy with me."

Grucca and Sarantain would have paid wages to show all of Waterfall the look on Bog's face.

"You pulled me from my rest for this? To use the word *snippy*?" Bog said, frowning to especially listen to her response so he wouldn't misunderstand.

"I called this meeting to determine if perhaps...someone... should draw her aside. I can't imagine the stress she's under."

"You wouldn't like to," said Bog.

"She saved my daughter. She can be snippy," said Sawyer Dotrig.

"If she goes under, Waterfall goes under. Shameful to say it, but that's the truth of it," said Tourmaline.

"Have they set about building trenches?" asked Bog. "Deep trenches?"

"No."

"I suggest they do so. Rows and rows of them at the village gate. Every slowed step is the possibility another of your citizens survives."

"What makes you think they'll come at the gate?" said Tourmaline.

"I've killed people like this Thief Mage before. Power seeks a front door to convince itself of its importance."

"Aye," said Grucca. "We could blaze pits of oil and release dragoons; he'd still come a'front."

"We can't evacuate," said Tourmaline.

"No," affirmed Bog.

"And no one will come to help," she said.

"Waterfall's past aggressions, of which I've heard plenty, have guaranteed that," said Bog.

Tourmaline, who in the past eight days hadn't slept much, dug her palms in her eyes and circled them, then let her face rest there while she thought. She was effectively running all of Waterfall, all to Khumalo's preferences. Part of her, a part she vilified daily, wanted to say this was Khumalo's fault, that if the Thief had been left a random person here and there, who would have known the difference in Waterfall's deaths and disappearances?

Part of her was learning magick.

She could hear that extra, resounding *k*.

Magick was something she never thought would be within

leagues of her life.

And yet it was the only part of her that felt real. Her official duties, though now diversified, were truncated things she ghost-walked through. Delegating was a wonderful thing. She'd pulled Deputy Cooney to the new position of Civil Preparedness; the woman's aptitude for strategic planning shone clear. Bethune credited himself by publicly acknowledging what had become known as the Emergency Sorcery Brigade, which consisted of twenty-odd parents and a few children wandering the village, mumbling odd phrases in various places. It seemed very much like praying, except the hand motions and finger positions looked very convincing.

Khumalo still wanted Amis and Amnandi under her observation, so Tourmaline rode to the little shack daily; there was room for another add-on at the other side of the home, but she didn't want to impose. Her brother was already there, and Sarantain, Bog, and Grucca camped out on the grounds every night.

Waterfall was not perfect. No place with more than two people was, and even two was a stretch. But to feel isolated and damned all in one breath was—it was—it was enough to make her eyes sting and her cover them with her hands till the feeling passed.

She implored Bog blearily, "*Talk* to her."

Khumalo, Amnandi, and Amis were at the moment gathering flowers, roots, fungi, and mosses.

Bog, tired of Tourmaline's green eyes on him, stood, sighed, and left the makeshift outdoor table and bench, stripping off his tunic as he went.

"Is that a yes... Is he going to..."

Bog's hands went to tug his breeches. The lukewarm water of the tub would do him nicely.

"Oh, dear," Tourmaline noted.

"Aye, he's always showing off his buttocks when the children aren't around," said Grucca. "Natural healing and whatnot."

She was taken with the play of his back muscles despite herself. Upper and much lower.

He climbed into the tub, leaned back with his arms over the sides, and presented his face's closed eyelids to the sky. He didn't seem angry, so Tourmaline took this as an elaborate yes that he *would* talk with Khumalo.

Warriors and witches were beyond dramatic.

***

"Words? Shall we have words again as we did on our ride back from yesterday's shopping?" Khumalo's brow arched high enough for another eye to fit under it.

"We said only what needed be said," Bog said.

"There is more?"

"There's always more, Ayanda."

The brow dropped. "All right."

"Recall that stream you took me to," said Bog. He slid his axe into his back sheath, his sword into the hip scabbard. "Ride with me there."

The sun shone clear and bright for a place meeting its doom. Had for days after the rain's passage. Bees, who never cared what humans or the preternatural did, carpeted the lush blue flowers edging the grass. They barely noticed the passing of the two horses except for a respectful dance in honor of the witch's forest maintenance. Human affairs were meaningless, but their deeds could be useful.

Khumalo and Bog slid down to walk their mounts.

"This will forever be one of my favorite places on Erah," said

Bog. "A nondescript piece of forest with small bell flowers, an open stream, and the scent of moss."

"You need no other stake."

"Country, title, or flag are as useful to me as a sword in my thigh." He led his horse to the stream's edge. The horse dipped to drink. Beedma followed suit. Bog picked out oval-shaped, flat rocks.

"You *do* know how to search out the rock formations?" Khumalo teased.

"Damn waterfowl." He handed Khumalo several stones. "The first time I did this, I thought it magick even though I knew the methodology behind it."

"Magick doesn't require ignorance to be magick." She skipped. Eight hops.

He skipped. Seven.

"Do you know you were followed by *two* ravens? One is tipped in gold, the other silver."

"They flew so high, I couldn't tell. Her sister."

Twelve skips from Bog. Ten from Khumalo.

Seven again from Bog. Seven from Khumalo.

"Waterfall's newest witch supreme wanted you to talk to me, yet we're throwing stones."

Bog looked for more. "Throwing's fun."

Khumalo grunted.

"You do that well," Bog said at the noise.

"Fine teachers."

He dropped stones in her waiting palm. "We've not known each other very long."

"There's a good chance we were friends in a previous life."

He smiled a bit. "I haven't asked the goddess about that."

"There is a theory that we are all things at all times. I may be the goddess."

"There are too many things and people I wouldn't wish to be." One of the stones in his rough hand had striations of tan against the warm slate. He tucked it into the tunic's inside pocket.

"I may be you on one of the stars out there," she said, though it was still too early for stars to shine.

"I'd hope you're doing a better job of it. How do you feel, Ayanda?"

"I have never been so frightened as when I saw in your head my daughter enshrouded by a thing that thought of her as nothing but food, and yet we think of half the visible world that way. Consumable. I'm not used to questioning why I'm here."

"I'm expert. Use me."

"I put her in danger; can you understand that?" Even the thought of the stones now felt too heavy in her hand. She dropped them. "That is nothing a child should ever experience, that sense of life being so entirely random that your own life is less than a whim. From the moment she drew breath, I have lived to destroy that whim." When she made eye contact with him, he would have cleaved half the sky to offer her the safer portion of it. "And I was not there to save her."

She stepped to him, laid her head on his shoulder, and cried.

Her headscarf smelled of clove and oil.

He did not embrace her, for that would have interrupted the flow of the connection she was making from him to the earth beneath their feet. She breathed against him, and he with her, until he quietly said, "Let your friends help you."

She drew back. "Those are not my friends, this smatter of people 'learning' magick. They think they are learning magick when all they're doing is appealing to unseen beings who appreciate politeness. This is a group of people who are going to go out into their woods and die unless I prevent it, yet they are hellsbound to feel they are doing something no matter if I attempt to dissuade them."

"How," he said into the space between them, "is that different from us?"

"Do learn to be silent, Bog of Nasthra. Hold me." Her arms wrapped around him. His wrapped around her. They breathed.

Eventually, they returned home to watch her daughter lead a small score of people in magick drills.

**

With every good meal, Bash's mind came back a bit. Thus far, they'd had three apiece. Trappers, wanderers, some smelling of the sea and spray of Waterfall, others of their need to find something meaningful apart from the community of humans fate tortured them with. Nine full of bones, spirit, and fear. Good, vital adults. Bash was a good hunter, too huge to move about quietly but big enough to sit unmoving, hunch as though a boulder, and draw curiosity.

The witch would have told the people within Waterfall to stay out of the woods, but meals were meals. Humans did only what they perceived three inches from their noses.

Raggle healed the slowest. Bash permitted the two to feed from him between human supper.

Perhaps nine more would do. Perhaps Bash could hunt closer to the village bit by bit. Twitswaddle didn't need full strength to move forward. There were three of them and one of her. One witch. And no matter that, from his hazy contacts with Raggle as she flared in and out of cognizance, the child was indeed a beast of worrisome proportions, she was still a child. Children could be turned aside by the proper distraction.

Would the witch's be any different? Twitswaddle wondered.

His decision: She would not.

✻✻✻

All along the mountain-facing areas of Waterfall, trenches were dug. Captain Pinyasama of the lucky feathered sarong lent her entire permanent crew to it. Trenches and pits. Anything to impede.

"If it seems a dragoon could climb out of it," she'd shouted, "it's not deep enough."

The guilds withheld aid, as they felt ill consulted.

The council stayed out of the way, as they did not wish to anger Mother Khumalo.

Nor anger Tourmaline, Amis, Gita, or Bettany, who had become something of a coven in behavior if not actual ability. Even in look a bit. Amis was never seen without a blue-black feather tied into her ratty hair.

The village didn't speak its mission but adopted a single goal wholeheartedly: kill three approaching monsters at its threshold.

Let there be no others.

Magic, demons, and nightmares would *not* come to disrupt Waterfall's ways.

Knowing when it would happen would've made things seem normal.

Khumalo knew where they were—Tourmaline knew that— but didn't want to attack them alone nor bring enough of a force to alert them in advance.

Plus, it would be far easier for Twitswaddle to seal himself in his own cave with its own protections than to draw him, the brute, and the wraith out in one clean swoop.

"Explosives," said Bettany's father, prepared to make them himself.

"Would cause a rockslide leading to a flood, leading to a

pestilence of dourflies it would take you several seasons to begin to eradicate," said Khumalo. "He chose well. I've considered every assault. This is not a hovel of bandits. Allowing them to come to us"—*rather than a mob thinking protection spells and house weapons will somehow prevail*—"will offer the most advantages."

Watchtowers, normally stocked with people who didn't care, were now stationed with people who didn't care but were too scared not to watch.

In a last-ditch effort of goodwill, Waterfall had sent messengers to neighboring Suod and Barrit to warn of "evils afoot," a message which reeked of guildspeak. Tourmaline had not approved that message to go out. Nor was it worth her recalling it. The mountain-facing side of Waterfall had been torn apart more effectively in five days than any of the wars or skirmishes ever accomplished. When this was over—and, by the mole over her heart, it *would* be over—repair budgets awaited, recriminations were guaranteed, and it would likely not be a bad idea for her to take up farming. On a big plot of land. With trenches around it.

Laughing at herself or fate or sometimes both gave her something to do besides fret. She didn't normally fret, but she performed it well nonetheless.

There was a lot to suddenly pulling a community together.

And the fact that this was not to be a drawn-out siege but a single decisive day sat extremely poorly on the stomach.

Constable Bethune approached. His stomach fared no better.

"Have you seen the old ones?" he asked, adding at her annoyed confusion, "Stepple. Orsys."

"Stepple was under your charge," she said. "No, constable. In all this"—she waved a hand sure to indicate general chaos and construction somewhere—"I have not noticed Orsys or Stepple."

"The stalls haven't shuttered. Matter of fact, the wharf's as normal as can be. Travelers, merchants, coins. The usual beggars are there. Not those two. Information you'd want to know towards passing along."

"Thank you, constable."

"This is madness, madam." He knew the teacher helping the carpenter spread dirt over thin plywood covering a pit just inside the village limit. The pit was as wide around as his house. Not far from those two, Captain Pinyasama's sharpest eyes and deadliest bowshots sent weapons up ropes to towers amid sharp cursing.

Tourmaline pointed out the captain herself doling orders as she strode the streets. "See her? She says she's fought magical beasts with her hands and her brain. Says the goddess favors those who don't want to fight but stand to deliver anyway."

"We could use a whole lot of that beneficence, then."

Tourmaline nodded. "Let us pray nonstop."

"The witch madam still supposed to give that talk today?"

"Yes."

"Life," he said, taking his leave, "has become interesting beyond belief."

***

Mother Khumalo found herself once again making use of the barrel and once again looking out over expectant faces. This small sampling of people willing to do what they could, even this least, to safeguard the most. If she'd felt pride toward them, it would have been a lie. It was kinship, simple, face-to-face, human kinship. She wanted no harm to come to them, and they, in their deepest hearts, wanted none to come to her.

And yet, even among this crowd, were those whose motivation grew from a desire to either control or harm others. Khumalo sensed it like an unwelcome odor.

For that reason, she decided to present facts as quickly and indisputably as she knew how.

"Understand this. When they come, they will think they can overrun me with your deaths. Deny them this advantage."

Khumalo stepped down.

Bog's frown began the moment Khumalo took that first departing step, Tourmaline's a moment after, and the two frowns met in the middle. Bog matched Khumalo's easy stride toward her horse and spoke at her shoulder. "Was that your rallying cry?"

"Better than shrieking the name of a goddess, yes?"

"I rarely— Yes," Bog caved.

"Grunt at them and tell them to get rest. Tell them to recite their protection spells at random. Tell them I am ready," said Khumalo.

"That's the speech you should've given them."

"They wouldn't have believed it of me."

"Why think they'd believe it of me, an outsider as much as you?"

"You fought alongside two of their own. Without any magicks. They need the certainty of that."

"I might have died if not for you," he said.

"They need that particular certainty, too." Khumalo mounted Beedma and rode off.

Tourmaline caught up. "Was that it?" she asked. She and Bog watched Beedma gather speed as rider and horse cleared the square.

"It was."

"May I borrow your horse?"

"Mamao is not for—"

Tourmaline was on her way to the horse's side. "Thank you."

It moved away from her a bit. Tourmaline remained purposeful. She trailed a hand from the midpoint of its neck to the saddle strap, hit the saddle once with a quick fist, then caught the bridle and jump-swung herself upward with a bustle of official skirts. She leaned her weight hard forward, gave the horse sharp jabs at the belly, and took off, hoping the high-alert atmosphere of the square and village proper would keep people spry enough to avoid injury, at least until she, too, cleared all traffic density.

When she did, she found out two things: Khumalo's horse was ridiculously fast.

But so was Mamao.

***

Khumalo didn't stop until well away from the village. When Tourmaline paralleled her, Beedma and Mamao nuzzled briefly before each settling into their horse thoughts while the two humans talked, horses being generally aware that humans talked a lot.

"I get asked several times a day by the guilds for an audience with you. I've successfully run interference thus far, but after that 'speech,' I seriously doubt there's any forestall left." She waited.

Khumalo said nothing.

"They...wish to voice concerns." Waited again. Even an acknowledgment there was a conversation being had would do.

Nothing again.

"They will now insist."

"By all the hells they will."

"They insist their funds should come with questions."

"I understood efforts were publicly funded."

"Yes, but—"

"I see you are understandably nervous. Rest easier. Tell your guilds the day I meet with them will be life-changing for them, and that they should be prepared for that."

"Specifically those words?"

"Specifically."

Tourmaline pressed for some sense of normalcy. "They consider themselves a huge portion of those public funds. And bedamned won't leave me alone."

"But we know they are not. No large community is pillared by the wealthy. This is fact on every continent of Erah. The wealthy exist as thieves and parasites. Would you prefer to relay that?"

"I would, actually, but I will not."

"Tourmaline...why do you bring this to me now of all times?"

"Because when this is over, they will take credit, and for them credit is powerful coin. None of the people who have wanted to learn from you deserve living under an ounce more weight from them."

Khumalo gritted her teeth. It had been seventeen years since she last gritted her teeth.

"I will meet. I'll require a candle."

"Witchery?"

"Of a sort."

Beedma's ears pricked up. *Witchery*, the horse knew, *indeed*.

***

There were seven faces in the small public room the following day. Not one of them was happy with the short notice, and even less so with the ceremony with which Khumalo placed a short white candle atop a clay disk on the lectern. She studied everything about the candle as she placed it, slightly furrowed her brow at it, and squinted ever so minutely, no doubt seeing if it was aligned with Erah in some way, as witches were wont to do.

Not a word had been spoken by anyone in the room, not even introductions. The tall witch had watched each guildsperson take a front-row seat. Literally, eyes on them until buttocks had found their final shape. Eyes as impassive as a massive brick wall in a narrow, foreboding alley.

Once all were seated, Tourmaline locked the door with a *click*.

The candle was a simple Waterfallian design. Dozens like it sold daily at a stall financed by one of the eldest of guildsfolk, Buford Rimes, not in attendance there but his nephew representing.

The seven breathed slightly easier at the familiarity of that one simple object. There'd be no magics.

Khumalo trapped the wick in her nails and twisted, shortening it significantly. She spoke a single clear word over it:

"Empaal."

Which sounded quite like *impale*.

Buttocks shifted.

"From the moment I light this candle, lives within this room begin to shorten. Speak succinctly, speak truly."

Fourteen eyes went to Tourmaline, who acknowledged not a single one.

Faster than the objections that wanted to fly from their mouths, the candle flared aflame.

Another elder guildsperson wasted no time. Her gravelly voice duly set the tone. "What guarantees have we that anything we've done will work?"

"That is a stance granted none of us," said Khumalo.

The gruff woman spoke again. "How will we know when they march on us?"

"We'll know."

A man who looked as though he awoke each morning red-faced and histrionic demanded, "How?"

Tourmaline shot Kieran Horne a warning glance.

"I have brokered assistance. I revise my statement. *You,*" Khumalo said directly at the man, "will not know. You won't be there." Khumalo regarded the entire room, hands behind her back, back as straight as ever, wondering who might broach the biggest question on each of their minds.

It was the nephew, a man whose fresh face and attention to coiffure screamed that he had been born to wealth and would die if dropped ten feet from its comforts. His eyes ran relay races from the candle to Khumalo.

"Show us what you can do."

Tourmaline dashed from her door station. "Madam is not here to perform for you."

"A demonstration is not a performance," said Kieran Horne, unasked.

"Nor is a demonstration called for," said Tourmaline. "I've seen firsthand what she can do."

Khumalo, like a teacher before a classroom, emerged from behind the lectern and stopped at the middle student in the line of seven, neither the nephew, the perpetual heart attack, or the elder, but a man more beard than face, more watchfulness than bravado, and more guile than decisiveness.

She spoke to him alone, but all seven were of one ear. "Shall I tell you how much life I've taken from you so far? Or would the assembled prefer a more-direct demonstration of mortality?"

"Not necessary, mum," said the red beard.

"I thought not." She turned and spoke to the candle. It went out. The silence of the room chilled despite the heat pouring in through its open, guarded windows. "I give you your portions back on condition: disappear or become useful. There is no mid ground. Comfort yourself with your wealth but disentangle from the lives of Waterfall."

"We employ those lives," said the bearded watcher.

"Perhaps they employ you. What use are you beyond serving as outlets for their waking hours? What use are you to yourselves beyond titles and acclaim? To insist I come before you to justify this community doing what they will without you is a foolishness you should never repeat with a witch in this life. Not all are as compassionate as I. Not all *beings* are as compassionate as I. Would you agree with this assessment, Madam Dotrig?"

"Unreservedly."

"There is one who has seen exactly what I am capable of and what I have faced, here, in your land."

"Mr. Bog," said Tourmaline. "You've noted him walking the wharf in precisely the manner an ancient oak does not."

"Do not insist on words with him. He eschews the warm glow of candles. I meet with you as a courtesy before battle and a warning following. My daughter has grown fond of several in Waterfall. Were she to return when she is older to find her friends lacking the warmth in their hearts she has come to expect, she would not be happy. You've already doubted my skills as a witch. My skills as a mother are entirely unknown to you. One hopes I'll have imparted to her a respect for restraint. If not that, then less a taste for judgement." She spoke to the candle again. "Empaal." It relit. "This meeting is adjourned unless there are further questions." The candle flickered, drawing each set of guild eyes to it.

"Nothing further," said the beard.

"Are you satisfied, then?" asked Tourmaline.

Khumalo waved the question into oblivion before a voice attempted—which they wouldn't—to answer. "We do not care if they are satisfied. Their given task is to be useful or remain unseen." A whisper in the room would have been a shout. "You may note by their silence we are all of accord."

With that, the flame stretched one final time before winking out on its very short wick.

"Meeting," said Tourmaline, "adjourned."

After each guildsperson filed out and the deputies were given the nod to disperse to do actual work, Tourmaline turned to Ayanda. "Do you know what frightened them most?"

"Enlighten me."

"You didn't let them speak."

"There are more than enough useless words in the world, wouldn't you agree?"

"With all my soul."

BATTALION

Amnandi's friends hadn't known she knew how to fight. Amis picked herself up, brushed herself off, and returned to the line.

Amnandi demonstrated the stance again. "Leading leg bent, stabilizing leg under you but slightly forward, shoulders aligned with the heel of the stabilizing foot. Arms reach forward, torso draws back, bent leg plants foot in opponent's sternum, and you let their weight carry you into a backward roll. If they hit the ground hard enough, you have several seconds to either attack or run away. Unina stresses running away." After seeing Bog practicing with his sword and axe at a young tree before he rode off—providing them plenty of firewood—Amnandi decided to forego magickal drills for physical. Piles of hay from the Dotrig farm served as safety matting.

Her friends, Amis included, albeit with bits of straw in her hair, mirrored her motions. If they were successful, she was of a mind to expand the class. Every child in Waterfall might come to excel at basic martial prowess.

That would be interesting. Some of them might even learn actual magick. Gita was already surprisingly proficient at protection spells and extending her consciousness a bit. If Amnandi stayed in Waterfall for a fair stretch, there was no telling the good to be done.

She hadn't been this excited since the sea voyage with Bog, which seemed a hundred years past.

They paired after three more form drills, this time Amnandi with Gita, Amis with Bettany. Each pair took turns throwing the other until all were dirty, sweaty, disheveled, and exhilarated.

"This will work on larger people?" asked Gita.

"With practice and sufficient motivation."

"I'm going to flip Da forever!" said Amis.

"You're so wicked," said Gita.

"He'll love it. Nandi probably throws her ma around all the time."

All four paused at the image. Giggling, then outright laughter, ensued, broken only by Bettany asking her two friends who had survived unspeakable danger—not that the girls had not spoken of it—

"How do you feel?"

Amis's usually raven-dark hair still seemed ashen, as if nothing would wash the experience away. Both she and Amnandi, to Bettany's eyes, even seemed older. Amis hadn't even shown them her scars.

"Hungry," said Amis.

"Well," said Amnandi.

Bettany nodded at this satisfactory conclusion of her evaluation and decided she wanted to throw Amis some more. Bog returned from the regular ride around an arbitrary perimeter he'd established. The girls waved and he, dismounting and removing his axe, saluted them with the heavy thing. Noting all the straw sticking from them head to toe, he called out, "You look like the foe of birds." He paused to observe, which delighted them because sometimes he gave them tips. They knew how to punch without breaking their hands, how to fall without absorbing the impact in all their bones, and how to stare someone in the eye as if the other person had never existed at all, that last coming easily to adolescents.

Bettany telegraphed her intention to throw Amis. Amis saw and agreed, letting the rough gray tunic Aunt Tourmaline had provided from one of the seamsters, with matching pants, be grabbed at the shoulders, her body get yanked forward, and Bettany's bare foot plant in her gut for the most fulfilling somersault ever.

Rolling to a stand, Amis and Bettany shared a single thought, and turned their standing recovery into an unbroken move of Amis now flipping Bettany.

They continued this over and over until they'd made a wide circle around their sparring area, by which time Bog had crossed the distance.

"Would this ever work on you?" Amis asked breathlessly.

"If you threw me, you'd have to take my axe. Those are the rules." The axe was as tall as she was and weighed twice as much.

"Those aren't the rules," said Amis. "Nandi, are those the rules?"

"I...have never fought someone for their axe."

"Amnandi is a creature of peace," said Bog, towering over Amis with a voice as though he knelt. "You and I are warriors." He proceeded into the shack, saw Ayanda Khumalo was in deep meditation, and left her undisturbed, sitting a while outside to watch the children's drills.

Would any one of them sit back at some point in their future lives and wonder had they ever been children at all? It was a jagged thought, and he had no desire their lives be burdened with jagged things. They were to grow older, make discoveries, and then grow old.

That would be the way of things. He swore it for Amnandi. He swore it for her friends, current and unmet. He swore it for Ayanda Khumalo.

Magicks were fine and good, but it was already proven even a wraith could succumb to a blade. If it took the right hands, he had two willing ones. If it took the right time, he had the days left to him to give.

The girls now alternated throwing one another in a cycle of continuous efficient motion. He became so enrapt, he didn't notice when Ayanda came beside him until she laid a warm hand on his shoulder. She sat with him. She watched.

"They are quite good," she said.

Bog wanted to squeeze her hand and wrap her in comforts.

"Yes," he said, a word that was generally an affirmation but in this case was flat and lifeless.

He wished he hadn't spoken. Saying no might've changed the future toward the better.

He wanted to say no.

But it wasn't possible to lie to the soul beside him. Not possible at all.

Nor wanted, come what may.

After a while, Khumalo said, "I know," to the no he left unsaid.

***

It has been said, Mother Khumalo wrote in the journal few

ever saw her write in, her daughter included, *that deeds beget deeds, punishments beget punishments, and violence begets the world. I do not believe in the last, despite the first being a given. I have had to vanquish revenants and thieves in Eurola when all I wanted was Erah's wonders to parade across my daughter's eyes. I've placed her in danger. Friends saved her, and I saved them. Deeds. But there is no guarantee which way a resultant deed will swing. An unsettling fact for anyone, but particularly myself. A witch. I am a being neither of the world nor in the world but made real by each. Given function, perhaps purpose.*

Perhaps *is a word full of possibilities.*

Perhaps the Thief Mage dies in his sleep. Or even has a dream which makes him cry, which erases his need for revenge. Perhaps the wraith considers fear—her own—a proper inducement to live out her life as a teacher. And perhaps the beast which the ravens have seen will allow me to tell it a story.

I think that unlikely. I do not do this for the people of Waterfall. I do this so my daughter—my world—will not arrive at the end of this set of deeds with tears in her eyes.

But if so...

If so.

May I be the one to wipe those tears away.

Always.

She placed the small notebook inside her robe, where it took up very little space at all.

The ravens had reported a sighting. The three were but a day away, the thief atop the brute's shoulder, the wraith a trailing cloud. Their slow approach wasn't of weakness but of purpose, cautioned the raven sisters. The three did not care that they were seen and did not try to run the ravens away.

It was surely as much a military parade as anything Waterfall had ever put on, thought Khumalo.

In twelve hours, she would leave to meet them.

A parade of one.

***

At eleven hours, she whispered to Amnandi, their foreheads together, a deep smile on both faces. At eleven and a half hours, she completed meditations, sat with Bog a moment, then tucked necessary items away within her robes.

As the twelfth hour came, Mother Khumalo climbed atop Beedma to conserve energy. It was sunny but not hot. Breezy but not blustery. An agreeable day for venturing, wandering, and exploring.

They rode in the direction of two very large circling birds.

***

Bash knelt and allowed Twitswaddle down. The mage operated under a spell casting himself in his finest in his mind's eye. This was called self-deception. He already had a plan to deceive his comrades for escape. This was unfortunate nature.

The actual grayed, dirty vestments nearly matched his brother's hide. Bash, forever naked, had never appeared clean in his life. Nor bright. Nor piercing except for his half-moon eyes, which never cast light during the day, meaning he was not piercing now. Simply lumbering.

There were times lumbering did precisely what higher purpose needed it to do.

Twitswaddle squinted against the sun, casting his paltry shadow backward onto Bash's waiting form.

Those damned birds. It was considered bad luck to kill them, a rumor he suspected they themselves promulgated. Circling and swooping, never landing to assume their diminutive forms, their bird mockery of those consigned to dirt. If he were close enough, he'd have loved to get his hands on one and throw it far into the nearest body of water—which would be yet another mockery.

Ignominy was endless in this world.

He frequently considered sending Raggle after them, but no, her strength was best used elsewhere.

The birds glided in wide, slow arcs as if made of nothing but time. He did not trust them, he did not trust the witch, he did not trust anyone anymore to respond as his station was due.

In his mind, he was a king. Crisp, close-fitting clothing to accentuate his physical presence in this world; the adopted name "Theophilus" to convey the gravitas lessers should acknowledge. In his mind, none questioned anything regarding him beyond what they might do to ease him. In his mind, he knew he was not truly a king, not a god...but he would never slide so low as to be merely a man. A fragile human dependent on the whims of others.

"Fetch us bears, Bash. Large ones if about. One final feeding, then vengeance, retribution, reclamation. Go swiftly. Find bears. Or humans. Beasts all the same."

During their later meal of thrashing bear, Twitswaddle noticed one of the ravens veering off and angling down, down, down until it popped out of view.

**

Mother Khumalo smelled the blood. The shrieking scent of it washed between tree trunks quicker than any forest fire.

Beedma got uneasy when she wore the mask, but carried her nonetheless. They stopped under a rustling dapple of leaves casting shadows. The hunter breathed easily. Breath was sight, breath was sound, it was the very engine of reality. She let the wind inform her.

The brute and the thief smelled like offal and loam, the revenant like absence.

They were close.

She hopped off Beedma and sent her walking back as they'd agreed. Her eyeless eyes had no need to look skyward to chart her course by the ravens.

Her urge was to run toward the miscreants. She fought it. She was where she needed to be. One or all three would eventually sense her. The thief would send the brute crashing through the forest in a show of intimidation.

Ayanda Khumalo had not yet been intimidated a second of her life.

***

Raggle sensed it: a blue energy leaching into the ground, attaching itself to the air, proclaiming itself a protector. The beast witch.

"A beacon is lit," Raggle rasped, slowly coiling around Twitswaddle's head.

"She thinks to toy with me." The Thief Mage drew himself to his full height. "Bash, do you have her?"

Bash drew a breath so deep, his ribcage neared popping. He exhaled a great, controlled stream and nodded.

"Let her know our stance on hubris. Taste the bones of a witch."

Neither the mountains nor the woods had heard Bash yell for longer than most had settled there. He threw back his head in anger for his brother, anger at the notion of being trapped on Erah for all his life, anger even at the goddess for not once having the courage to show herself to him. Demons beget gods, not the other way around! He was Bash of the Seventh Underlayer. He was the bone grinder and the lament, the hunger and the blind satiation. A roar from him ripped holes in time and space. It killed stars and snapped backs.

The roar, a blast like boulders clattering down a dragoon's spine, sent birds aflight, deer scrambling, and hearts pounding, and when the roar faded to a gargle in Bash's thickly veined throat, the demon pounded the earth with his elephantine feet and ran, snapping young trees with his shoulders, throwing up great gouts of sod with every footfall. It felt good to ram his way through the world again.

It would be even better to rip the arms from one who opposed him and snack while their eyes lamented the precise moment of their birth.

Twitswaddle and Raggle followed the destruction appreciatively at a slow pace.

YIELD

Khumalo felt Bash's vibrations and rose to meet him at a run. Beneath her robes she was wrapped neck to ankle in leather bands hard as armor but restricting her motions not at all. Where Bash left deep footprints in his wake, she barely touched the ground, zigzagging between trees and around obstacles with a speed and ease which amazed even the ravens. The birds did their best to follow the combatants inward, to calculate their moment of crossing, but Khumalo was too swift and random, leaping now at a tree and climbing to a high branch she immediately leapt from, and kept leaping, tree to tree without pause, until a final leap angled her downward, where Bash would have raced past had she not raked him across the shoulder, throwing him off balance face first into a tree. He rebounded from it and came around reaching for her, but she slid under his legs, snagged the trunk with her claws, and used the momentum to swing around and land on his back, reaching around to dig her fingers into his chest and draw them back, leaving thin welts with the barest dribbles of milky white blood, then somersaulting to a crouch behind him, where she swiped an X across the meat of his back.

Bash touched his chest. He brought a finger to his nose, to his lips, finally his sandpaper tongue. He couldn't recall the last time he'd bled. Not even the thrashing bears had broken his skin. The witch waited just out of reach, the balls of her feet ready to carry her in any direction. She was nimble.

The skulls of nimble things made for welcome treats.

He took a step toward her.

She moved back.

Another step. Another move.

A deep growl built from Bash's depths to the curled lip on his face, where it hissed out like rocky steam.

His huge body lunged into a run.

Her lithe did the same. Toward him, hands in the billows of her sleeves.

In a blink, she had weapons, gleaming compact scythes with handles she clicked together and swung at him in a motion so fluid, he barely followed the sequence of events. Instinctively, though, he noted the blades possessed the same unseen blue energy as she, and he slammed a foot to try to stop his meeting her stroke.

The strike opened a gash across a forearm, a ribcage, and a palm.

Bash wailed in anger.

"This can end here, beast," the witch shouted over its ire, ripping the words from her throat. "I...know...your intent. Do not test me."

Bash would not lower himself to speak language with this witch. She may have spoken with the sound of a beast, but she knew nothing of the ways of beasts. She would know his words by his fingers wet with her windpipe in his hands.

He bent and dug great clumps of earth with both hands, flinging them with enough force to break bones. In blocking it with her slashing blades, she was momentarily blinded. He leapt and swung and connected with a satisfying shatter.

But it was not her. Shattered bark jutted outward from the tree behind her.

She, in a perfect split, was on the ground, her torso on level with his shin bones. She thrust the blades forward in a double-armed push. They barely dug in, but dig in they did.

She yanked back as his fists raised to hammer down, cast a portal behind herself, and fell in. Erah trembled when he struck.

She reappeared a fair distance from him and removed her mask. "Yield!" His only answer, a rumbling dash toward her. She replaced the mask, readied her stance, and easily pivoted when he threw himself at her.

The slash at his inner knee drew a howl of pain. That his blood looked like the sap from the milkweed fascinated her, but this was not the time to be fascinated. Blood poured down his leg, but rather than drop or yield, he forced himself around on his good leg with the long sweep of his arms extended to either catch her up or deliver a blow. He snagged a colorful sleeve on a ragged nail, enough to draw her off balance, enough to pull her toward him, enough to open his mouth as wide as could be, wide enough to fit her entire head inside for a decisive bite while in an embrace meant to snap her spine...but for the fact that she swept her enchanted blade upward and lodged it in his gut, creating a momentary barrier between them which Bash looked down at in surprise, looked at her with both hatred and curiosity, with the realization that each time the blade tasted him, it went deeper for a taste of more.

More was what he, Twits, and Raggle lived for, not that it be reversed upon them. Wounds were for the weak to consider as they fell to those who hungered.

The witch stepped back, pulling the weapon with her. Blood spurted once as though released to play. She turned away. A hole in reality appeared before her. She entered and was gone.

Khumalo appeared before Bog outside the village gates.

"Stand ready," she said, a harsh growl but clear.

She reappeared before Bash.

Bash ran at her.

A portal opened.

She sidestepped the brute.

When Bash blinked next, he stood before a large man with a large axe gripped in both hands. Two large men were with him. All of them were armored, and each's weapon—only to Bash's attuned eyes—glowed lightning blue.

Many yards behind the men: a child of similar cloth as the witch chanting and making finger motions. Far behind her, a row of people mirroring her words and actions.

Around Bash, no Twitswaddle or Raggle.

Deep in his brain the brute formed the emotion that communicated the three words of all reality:

So be it.

***

In the forest, Twitswaddle listened for sounds of battle. Nothing. He watched the treetops for violent swaying, tried his best to feel the sudden quieting of subtle energies announcing the death of an impediment.

It had been quiet for longer than it needed to be, but the energies persisted.

He motioned Raggle to him. "Fly. Kill the witch."

"Should we not be together?"

"I am not as healed as you and you not as injured as you believe. You're swift, though, and she cannot be as swift as thee. Hold her fast. Bind her. Feed until you are a star turned night. I'll arrive to impart the death stroke."

"And of our brother?"

"If he be harmed, her last breath, sister, shall be his balm."

Raggle's slow swirling around his body extended its orbit with each lie spoken, so expansive that she resembled a storm and he its calm center.

She turned possibilities over in her mind. Stratagems and intentions. The witch had harmed her. That was natural cause for death. The amount of suffering, however, required due consideration.

And then Raggle had it.

And, in a blur, was off.

She found the witch because the witch wanted to be found.

But she did not stop. Overhead and out of reach, Raggle blew by the woman's defensive stance without slowing, her speed so great, she was but a smudge.

Straight for the port and sea. Straight for succulent, full Waterfall and somewhere in there a witch's child to continue a feast.

Khumalo called silently to the ravens: *Drag her back to me.*

***

Khumalo had asked that Bog first ask it to yield. He did so out of deference but swung his axe at the same time since he knew the answer.

In rearing back to evade the blow, Bash put himself in line

with Grucca's and Sarantain's flashing blades on either side of him, each slashing at a raised forearm but doing little damage.

The realization pinged somewhere deep in Bash's brain: they were weaker than the witch. He stepped back, roaring as he thumped his scaly chest a single time with enough force to crack stone. The three humans kept him within a triangle but maintained their distance. He watched them, they watched him.

White, thick blood poured from him in key spots.

Answering with a roar of his own, Bog swung his fine axe, which did have a name, in a flywheel. The thing stood several heads above him and was twice his thickness. It looked like the spawn of a shark and bad decisions, except it had the huge, misshapen grinding teeth of a human, which rendered it more grotesque.

There was an old saying about how one ate a dragoon. Bite by bite. Yes, it was sacrilege to say so.

These were not devout times.

The thing gave ground before the heavy blade. Its rear leg, however, *continued* into the ground. Half that leg was swallowed. Its body fell backward, pinning its form crosswise against the hole and the splintered wood and dirt falling in on it.

Bash roared. The human with the axe ran toward him, screaming the name of a goddess Bash had not heard in a long time, but he remembered she was not always kind.

Bog leapt atop the thing's chest and raised Ghostface toward its head. They met eye to eye that moment. It was not a moment of hesitation; it was a moment of knowing. One of them would die.

Bash flailed. His tree-trunk arm connected with Bog's side, sending Bog flying. Bash sensed the satisfying crack of bone even before the butterfly child turned at the human's wail of pain to speak words in his direction. The man calmed, got to his feet with a grimace, and picked up his axe.

Bash climbed out of the hole and was met with two ineffectual running slashes across his back by the others. He ignored them to run toward the axe man...

...and bounced off a pocket of air, just slightly but enough to puzzle him, until it dawned: magicks. The worst of them, the small, affronting kind only the weak cloaked themselves in. His eyes went to the child leading the group of bones behind her. Bash pushed through the solid nothingness, angling toward the small one.

An axe flew and buried itself in its shoulder.

Grucca and Sarantain moved in, swinging high, swinging low, their blows rewarded with trickles of blood. They met behind the reeking bulk to go for the milk-covered leg.

Bash twisted. He caught Grucca by the arm and prepared to bite down.

A sword jammed into its mouth dissuaded it. Sarantain saw the merest tip of his blade protruding from the thing's cheek. He pushed.

The eyes of the thing became full moons.

It released Grucca to grab at the sword, snapping it once freed of its mouth and throwing the halves at the fleeing men.

The axe clattered out of its shoulder.

Bash looked dimly at it a moment. He picked it up. He had never used a weapon in his life, had never needed to. Humans relied on them, but humans were small and fragile, the smaller, the more the need. He felt the ensorcelled power of the thing tingling his calloused palm.

Humans were but naked wisps without their weapons and their magicks. Gristle, marrow, and fear.

He advanced on the thrower with it. The other two, now at a safe distance, produced crossbows from their backs, nocked quickly, and fired. The tips lodged loosely on either side of his head. He brushed them away and continued toward the wisp that angered him the most. To chop him into sections would be satisfying, and then to separate the meat from the bones even more so. And once past him, Bash would be within Waterfall once again. His sludge brain nearly wept at the thought. Bones to last for years! A fitting feeding ground, one to surpass even the old days.

Bash decided to keep this axe when this was over, perhaps wear it around his neck. A wisp shown that its weapons meant nothing became nothing.

Bash slammed into two more pockets but pressed through. It was only a matter of time before the standing human ran.

Bog did run.

Toward Bash.

This one was a fool, Bash decided, a fool damaged beyond reckoning. A bull, no matter how enraged, never charged a giant. There was an order in things.

Bash raised the axe to remind the human.

He swung for the human's neck.

Amnandi appeared from an electric hole faster than the swing, simultaneously throwing a portal before Bog, which they both entered, exiting behind Bash.

Amnandi, heart pounding, immediately vanished.

Bog drove his hands into the gash behind Bash's left knee and grabbed for anything he could find, be it meat or bone. The leg gave out amidst the beast's howl, trapping Bog's hands and pulling him against its body.

Then it gave a great push backward with its good leg, sending both bodies into the air. Bringing both bodies down.

Itself on top of Bog.

Even the farthest protection caster heard the wail and explosive loss of air.

Bog's eyes closed. He forced them open. Saw the sky was as high and as blue as it ever was. Knew that between the clouds and himself lay a million breaths. He had to take but one.

He snatched it inward. He threw long arms around the beast's neck. He locked his bloodied hands with his elbow at the thing's windpipe, for even demons drew air. Muscles straining their most, he squeezed.

Grucca and Sarantain moved in to occupy its arms with swords. It kicked its massive leg at them. It bucked.

The humans refused to stay in one place for longer than a swordstroke. Their blades whirred like wings.

Welts became scratches, scratches became cuts, cuts became something Bash's brain had not processed in forgotten ages. Fear. Bash rolled to his side, lifting the unyielding human upward, now with enough space between the human and the ground to slam toward the hardpacked dirt and turn the man's body into a sack of broken stones. Bash fell.

And continued to fall. From a great height.

There was a child on his chest.

He plucked the child up and stared at her.

There was a man on his back, now trying to break his neck rather than choke him.

Cold wind whistled by all of them.

The man kicked a boot as close to the child's reach as he could. She immediately grabbed inside, retrieving a dagger, and spoke a word the blade agreed with, for it entered the thick gray flesh as easily as a serpent's tooth.

The hand released the child. The wind took her.

Bog caught a tumbling view of Amnandi billowing away like a colorful flag grown wild. The next moment their eyes locked, he felt the static buzz of the portal at his back, felt her arms around his neck. He let go of Bash and free-dropped.

He and Amnandi landed rolling, Bog cocooning Amnandi; they slammed into bales and bales of hay outside the stables near

Nowhere.

Amnandi wasted no time in throwing another portal, taking them back to the village gates.

Above them, the comet that was Bash of the Seventh Underlayer continued to fall, so fast and definitively, the assembled barely had time for two blinks before the impact.

"Back to your friends," Bog told her. He didn't wait to see if she complied. Sarantain threw him an unbroken sword. Bog caught its hilt, and strained to keep his arm from shaking wielding it. He advanced on the slight crater where even now the beast stirred. *Why did damned things hold so much life in them!* he railed.

'Twas then that the wraith, trailing ichor in the sky, raced overhead, straight for the group of protectors.

Khumalo, on the wraith's tail, ported atop the village belltower and threw a double-bladed lance through her.

The wraith, jetting new tatters and liquids, did not falter.

It flew straight for Amnandi. Beside her, Amis. Behind them, Gita and Bettany. Behind them, people who amounted to prayer warriors.

Khumalo ported to Amnandi and threw up a protection spell, which the wraith slammed into and tried to flow over.

Mother Khumalo extended the spell outward. Amnandi picked up on the energies used and assisted. A bubble enveloped Khumalo and the children. The wraith enveloped the bubble.

All was darkness except the pulsing blue sigils of Mother Khumalo's mask, brightening and fading in sync with her efforts.

Then, through the gray and the oil and the smoke and the filth, human fingertips. Human hands clawing, pulling pieces of the wraith away.

Raggle twisted from the shield in a blanket around these new humans, constricting as powerfully as she could. One, a green-eyed female, spoke muffled words Raggle had heard the witch say mere minutes before in the woods, and her constriction faltered.

She whipped her ragged self away before the witch's claws found their mark.

Khumalo saw that Tourmaline and Sawyer Dotrig stood but wasted no thought on them. The wraith made fast for the crowd, piercing protection spells along the way like bubbles, yet visibly affected by each.

She was not an avenging storm but a pale, unkempt ghost.

An elder stepped out from the crowd. Then another.

Elders, often foolish, carried the most delicious fears.

Raggle pierced one—not a feeding but a flash of healing—and looped into the other, racing high into the sky before the witch reached her.

There would be no peace until she killed the witch. She could not kill the witch until she killed the child. Snap the heart in two.

Raggle flew to Bash, broken, half-dead bone eater Bash still struggling to put off the death blow coming to it. She made of herself a whirling mass of talons and teeth, stretching her form to her limits, driving the humans back while allowing some of her energy to leech into Bash, just enough that he might stand and be of use.

Where in all the hells was Twitswaddle?

She stopped herself thinking. What use were rhetorical questions when blades were in play?

Instead, the anger to the answer in that question fueled a lashing from her that caught the human who had dared lay injury on her first, the scar-faced bowman, square in the chest, leaving a smoking hole through tunic, under-armor, and skin beneath.

Arise and be trouble, she sent to her brother, fleeing the reprisal.

Bog went for the throat.

So did Bash.

In this instance, Bash was faster. He rose slowly, Bog dangling by his throat.

And Bash, for the first time in his life, spoke to a human in a language no human had ever heard.

"How many times can you stab me before I snap your neck?"

Bog thrust.

Pressure increased to breaking on his neck. He was vaguely aware of the beast, caring little for the blows of Sarantain, lifting him even higher in triumph.

Blood felt as though it should geyser from Bog's ears. There was no room for even a thread of breath to travel his throat, let alone allow for an appeal to the goddess. It was just as well. The goddess knew his heart as well as his life. Death presented no need to speak to one another.

Bog tried to thrust again, but there was no longer strength to hold the sword. It fell from his grip as both arms went slack.

Awareness left him as his soul took Bash's hold to be the goddess coiling around him.

Then all was quiet. Very still.

Even the fetid warmth of Bash's breath against his face was gone.

And now, a sensation of falling.

But rather than an unending pit for those who had dishonored themselves, merely a short fall to the ground.

Air, air which felt as though formed of wild boars and nettles.

And standing only because of its position and balance of its tree-trunk legs, the beast: its eyes closed as in repose, its insatiable jaw slack, a hole of glowing blue edges where a good portion of its upper chest should be. This was where the distant forest shone through.

At its feet, a little girl in reds and blues, her fingers trembling even when she dropped to her knees to lay hands on Bog's throat, chest, and forehead. Bog felt that trembling and knew that it would never leave her even if it left her. She had learned to fight, all the way to the point of killing. Khumalo had told him of a previous home being burned, of how it had left a wound of mistrust in the world in her daughter.

Bog knew he wasn't dying and knew he would talk with Khumalo about this. It was very unlikely her daughter would never be burned from a home again.

But for now, Amnandi worried about him, and he cried. He cried for several reasons, but mostly that she cried for him.

REFUSAL

The delivery boy refused to die poor. He refused to leave Erah as "the delivery boy." That most of his clientele didn't know his name made him hate them more and, in hating them, serve them better, for if they paid well enough for him to drain their pockets, he would gladly sit below their crotchline with a bucket. That he might die committing one of these illicit affairs never crossed a thought enough to bother him. He might die of a sting, a fight, slip, an unmended heart, or the best night of his life. Maybe get his flame pinched for waiting for crazed wizards.

Thinking about any of them didn't change anything he could do about the end.

Knowing this was the last that the good coin of the crazed wizard would trade hands was worth a thought or two to McConnell Lourde.

All he had to do was get him to a boat undetected. *Undetected* was not the wiry boy's middle name—it was *Pitch*—but it *was* the motivating component of his life. That and knowing where to be for messages and signs from needful things.

He hadn't, however, planned on having to clean him up so thoroughly, but he'd had a feeling.

He shaved the wizard's face, holding his breath as much as possible. The mint leaves he'd given the old man to chew weren't doing much.

As more of his face unscruffed, the narrow, craggy face looked almost official, like he should've sat as a guildsperson who never uttered a word but always communicated his intent.

And, as no one would've let him on their ship looking as he did when the delivery boy met him in the woods, he had estimated the wizard's size and brought him the cleanest clothes he could "procure" from a finery shop: red vest, black shirt with the ruffled wrists that nob types seemed to prefer, black trousers, and brown boots—the boots ill-fitting, but they would do—and a draping, gray, floral-embroidered coat which seemed equally wizardish. He hadn't bothered with underthings. If anybody got that close to the wizard, it was their misfortune to bemoan, not McConnell's.

He scraped the razor up the wizard's neck toward his chin, not even thinking of how easy it would be to kill him and take his entire purse. It never paid to kill the strange or the supernatural. Had a way of coming back on you.

He made the final rough stroke. Shaving dry was a chore but it was done. He picked up a jug of water and indicated the wizard should stick his head out as far as possible. Maybe the water would carry away some of the dirt and oil and twigs and living things. Take the stench downwind.

It wet the shoulders and collar of the clean clothes, but they'd dry by the time McConnell's small, agile wagon reached its final destination.

Why the old man wanted to leave by the southern port of Barrit, McConnell didn't know. Also didn't care.

As they made the short march to where McConnell had hidden the horse wagon, the delivery boy remarked to himself that the old man had more pep in his step than might have been imagined.

***

Khumalo retrieved her mask from where it had fallen. *Detached* was the more accurate word, and it had never done that in her life. But then, she had never done to another what she did to the wraith.

Pieces of Raggle were strewn from watchtower to pit to hay wagon to ground. Only one still moved, the one pulsing irregularly in her other hand, a piece which she very carefully slid into the hollow of the mask, raised the mask to her face as though it were a chalice, and spoke words into it, nearly a whisper, but Amnandi—who had rushed to her mother's side—heard. The tears the young one cried for Bog were joined by fresh ones for her mother.

Amnandi remained quiet, though.

The mask spoke the wraith's true name back, in Ayanda's mind, in the wraith's tongue. This name was Ayanda Khumalo's property forever. The mask allowed no spells of forgetting.

Vanquishing a foe was one thing. Decimating them, another. Ensuring there was no possibility for release of spirit from *any* part of Rabinandrath Night, formerly feared as "Raggle," was unforgivable.

To each shred torn from the wraith, Khumalo'd uttered words of sealing, trapping tatters here, bones there, the head, the heart, the talons and teeth, in perpetual concealment from any notion of self the wraith had ever had.

And now, trapped in the mask, the brain. That which bound the unrepentant beast together, a purple thing of tiny ruptures and metallic tendrils reaching for each other, never the same configuration from moment to moment, but always hungry.

Khumalo turned away from all and hunched over to conceal from anyone the pocket dimension she was creating. The human eye was ill equipped to see such nothingness without harm to the psyche.

A witch was born to it.

She placed the mask inside.

As the dimension sealed, she dropped from the hunch into a sitting position, her head dropped and arms crossed to hide her face.

The change—the return—happened quicker without her bond to the ancestral mask.

She stood a few breaths later, mostly Ayanda Khumalo, and faced Waterfall.

Amnandi took her hand and guided her inward. Tourmaline fell in step beside them, Grucca propped by Sarantain after and, approaching, a frightened group of people speaking words of protection, words they uttered even more so when they reached Ayanda Khumalo, hoping to heal every obvious pain she bore. Protection without compassion was worthless.

It was a magick each came by themselves.

Khumalo became vaguely aware of their presence only when they pressed in. "Tend to the dead," she said.

"You're injured," said Tourmaline.

"Which means I am not yet dead and my deeds not yet in need of comforts." To no one in particular, she said, "Tend to those who cannot tend themselves."

The crowd loosened. A few remained near her. Most dispersed, seeking the fallen.

Raggle had been indiscriminate. She hadn't taken many, but she had done so decisively.

"Take me away from here," Khumalo said to Tourmaline before dropping to sit beside Bog, who knew not to attempt to move even if he could. Khumalo glanced at the tumult around her and sighed.

Tourmaline found Bethune in the crowd. She motioned him over, gave him instructions which he hurried to carry out, and she, spotting her niece and her niece's friends standing hesitantly but ready at the fore fringe of the crowd, plopped beside the tired maternal witch and gradually, consciously, matched her breath for weary breath.

**

Anything that didn't hurt, throbbed. Bog had never had a demon smoosh him before.

Ayanda had enough cuts, scrapes, and bruises to look as though she'd done heavy calisthenics in a bramble patch.

The elders who had died, wife and husband Aileen and Faber Derry, were returned to their family with all due solemnity and more silence than was normal from a family.

Bog assumed all the dead had received the same quiet delivery and silent reception. What had happened was a thing no merchant, laborer, child or elder should have words for.

Magick and battle should have been things solely of fiction.

This was day two of Bog's three-day recuperation in Mother Khumalo's infused tub. The protection spell she had personally spoken over him saved him from major breaks. Speaking still hurt, so he wrote everything, although with Ayanda he was able to use a sign language taught early to everyone back home. Moving very gingerly. Anything emphatic he left to Tourmaline to read from

Amnandi's chalk tablet.

"*What reason do you have to leave now?*" she read.

"You were the first to ask where was the thief in all this," Ayanda said to Tourmaline rather than answer her question.

"He stole from us again," said Tourmaline.

"Yes, he did."

"He took no hostages, threatened no one here. He is gone. Leave him that way," said Bethune. He had taken to loitering around Khumalo's home.

"That makes him all the more a danger to others," said Khumalo.

"I can come with you," said Tourmaline.

"There are those who love you. Stay and discover them."

"Do you require my ship?" said Captain Maab Pinyasama, there to see Grucca's improvements herself. And not "a" ship; the offer already made and sealed.

"It's the fastest," croaked Grucca.

"And best crewed," said Sarantain.

"We need to get to him before he makes landfall," said Khumalo. "He would not simply relocate a village away, not after all this. He seeks to put distance between us."

An intercontinental voyage, Bog signed.

Ayanda nodded.

"Where?" asked Tourmaline. Options were limited. This time of year, no one sailed toward Plitta. The open waters were too stormy. Icy Fap was a wasteland. Tish was huge, almost as big as Afrela, but Afrela was closer. A thief could lose himself anywhere along Afrela's coast, even a pale, wizened one.

"Afrela," said Mother Khumalo.

Bog signed, *He will not stain its shores.*

"This is promised," said Khumalo.

Afterward, during a quiet moment away from everyone else,

Tourmaline cornered the witch. "We've got many injured. No one can tend them as you."

"Amnandi can."

"A child..."

"She has seen death. She must now reacquaint herself with life. Have your physicians tend them as well, but don't let them get in Amnandi's way."

"And if you can't find him? The *Bane* is a fast ship, but it's not lightning. You'll be gone a long time."

"Not long."

"Ayanda..." Tourmaline gave up. The logic from the witch was there, just not meant for an administrator from a well-established trading port to grasp yet. She'd learned one iron fact about this rigid woman: she did not do things that didn't need to be done. "Safe journeys."

"You understand why I must do this?"

"No. There are more evils in our world than blades of grass, and you're chasing this man clear across it. Why?"

"I am aware of this one."

***

Khumalo sailed on the third day.

What she said to Amnandi before she left:

"I will never ask a promise of you that I would not make myself, and so I promise I will return to you fully intact with arms wide. Watch over Bog. Continue your friends' educations."

What was signed to Bog: *Be here when I get back.*

Instructions she left on Tourmaline's shoulders: "Find any who are missing. Diligently care for all who are hurt."

Words she said to Sarantain, who kissed the love of his life and left with her: "Thank you."

"Been a while since we had an intercontinental voyage," said Captain Pinyasama, welcoming someone as color-laden as she aboard. "The *Bane* will do good by it. Strengthen her resolve."

"He has three days' head start," Sarantain noted, "and the seas leave no tracks."

"We have friends," Mother Khumalo assured.

***

She saw what fascinated Amnandi about being on a ship, or perhaps *this* ship, as they had been on many vessels. The *Bane* sped along as though traveling atop pure thought. The sea could become blue, or gray, or a dancing silver, and yet was ever the sea. It spoke its moods plainly. This wasn't communication one received on land, even for witches. *Perhaps*, Khumalo thought, *this is why searavens claim their space so fiercely.*

This ship's captain was practically half-bird and sang to herself a lot between sharp orders and sharper observations of the sea's relation to sun, sky, and the omnipresent wind, increasing the ship's speed with each subtle alteration in course. Not a single feather from her long sarong ever blew off as she climbed, marched, and sighted all over the pristine decking of the finest ship likely ever introduced to Erah's veins.

The crew all had the necessary eyes of merchants but also the keener vision of explorers. They pointed out things to each other that each had surely seen a million times before, but did so with such enthusiasm, it made pods of large somersaulting fish, or octopods riding underwater twisters to the surface in a whirl of arms, renewably fascinating.

***

On the second day of sailing, she allowed Stepple and Orsys to make their presences known.

"Captain said we could stay on board till all that was over," said Stepple.

"You were scared," said Khumalo.

"Yes. Then you came on board and we knew it wasn't over." He looked on the verge of crying. Khumalo wrapped him up, cradling the back of his head in her hand.

"I apologize to you, my friend."

"We was scared, Madam," he said. "What could we do?"

"You've done more than you need."

Orsys moved a step, then closer, then burrowed herself directly into the press of bodies, and they all stayed like that while the warmth of the sun mingled with the cool of the breeze. Khumalo hoped the goddess heard her thoughts of sorrow for them.

***

She was forced, gently, to have a meal in the captain's mess the following night.

"Your daughter, I will adopt should anything happen to you. Tell me about yourself, Ayanda Khumalo of Insheree."

"I am the third of three children but treated as the oldest since five. My soul has been tied by love once. I rarely talk about myself because I'm a story I've already lived; I'd much rather hear yours told without you telling. Amnandi has been teaching me to live in multiple planes as she does. It has increased my perceptions many times over. I will never turn away a sweetbread or a hug from her. I've dreamt of the future. There are things called 'cars' and 'smog' coming. Perhaps I can prevent that. In the very far future, Erah will merge with a world called 'Earth.' I cannot prevent that, and in a way it seems necessary. I like people who reserve a portion of their beauty for random, unknown encounters, like the way your skirt fascinates me. But they must also reserve some for themselves. I had a lover who massaged my feet so expertly, it was nearly sculpting; I told her this. There is a statue of me in Denebral. Amnandi's father—that tethered piece of my soul—is perhaps the best person I have ever known. If there were to be immortals, he would be among them. At night, when I'm dreaming and he's listening, I make sure to dream Amnandi as well. She is my sweet. She is my exploration. I already know if she were to call you mother, I would be pleased." Khumalo's eyes smiled sadly at the captain. "Is that enough?"

The captain reached across and gathered Khumalo's fingers into a squeeze. "It serves you well. It's you to the core. You should definitely go back to being her when this is all over."

"You're extremely perceptive, Captain."

Maab drew Khumalo's hand upward for a respectful kiss on its warm back. "I surround myself with perceptive people. Keeps me alive."

***

"Hand me the loud box," said Captain Pinyasama. The ravens had advised to look for a passenger ship whose fore and aft were emblazoned in the brightest white. The ship in white continued its attempt to tack away. "Captain of pursued vessel, I am not familiar with you. I am Captain Maab Pinyasama. If you are familiar with me, raise all sails to conserve energy on both our parts. I bring you no ill." She lowered the box to await a decision.

First one sail, then another, finally all raised. Maab imagined the other ship's crew cursing her name in multiple languages.

She gave the order to pull alongside, and from there shared the signals with the other captain to request boarding under peaceful colors. The colors were sacrosanct whether merchant, passenger, warship, or pirate filth. One might deceive without colors, but once colors were flown, there was no greater honesty found along the length and breadth of the entire world.

As the requesting ship, all mooring ropes were the *Bane*'s, as was the crossing plank. Water encouraged economy and necessity. If for any reason there was cause to cut ropes or hack plank, the accommodating ship certainly wouldn't incur the supply loss.

Sarantain and two others crossed first, received the captain's respect, and took up watchful positions. Maab followed next, spoke briefly with the captain—a small man very tired around the eyes—and gave the hand signal for Khumalo to board.

The ships might have rested on hardwood as Khumalo strode the plank between.

One of Sarantain's mates, a woman whose demeanor spoke to closed doors being things to smash through, automatically extended a hand to help Khumalo down the set of steps placed at the foot of the plank, as though Khumalo were royalty. Khumalo took her hand, gave it a slight squeeze of thanks, and stepped surely onto a ship that equally surely quartered one of the last of the most pestilent people on Erah. In attempting to escape he had set the perfect trap for himself. She had but to collect.

"I am told," the world-weary Captain Malokofsky of the *Dragoon's Rest* said confidently upward to her; his eyes informed her he had a home to go to, a loved one to hold, and perhaps a handful more voyages between the permanence of that joy, "that you operate under seal of law. That I have on this ship a person of great interest to you. Captain Pinyasama is not known for frivolousness. Describe this person to me."

"In want of sun even if bathed in daylight. Likely dressed in puffery."

"Narrow it down a bit, madam."

"A bald man with a perpetual air of hunger. He will be furtive in crowds, bold as a king alone."

"And you've not made shore since leaving port?" said Maab.

"Not once."

"He is a mage," said Mother Khumalo, "perhaps capable of misdirecting the eyes of others to a small degree."

"But not yourself."

"Not myself." She produced the small, sealed scroll that Tourmaline had assured her she'd need. "Affidavit of charges from the constabulary of Waterfall."

"Bethune? I know Bethune. Bethune the buffoon."

"I will not call him that."

"Thank you." The captain took a split second to calculate every variable available. "I give you an hour to find your mage. My ship is no place for battles, magical or otherwise."

Khumalo felt the sacred surge of the sea, felt the press of life within it. Perhaps the goddess herself had slowed the waters surrounding the pristine ship carrying people to and fro across her world. There would be no battle. She nodded assent, then set out, Sarantain trailing her.

She didn't hurry her search. Instead, she studied faces. Ships were worlds, and each world differed as much as stars differed from planets, planets from moons, and moons from the unknowable dark of the sky. The crew's faces on this ship held one thing in common with their captain: they were tired. Tired of sailing dreams around the world but partaking in none of their own. They functioned well; the ship was clean and repairs made to appear seamless. Its passengers were well behaved, as being foolish on the open sea had the clear potential of turning one into a shark's next meal.

The ship took on twice as many passengers as its total crew. Khumalo had already estimated twenty-five crew. Most of its fifty passengers continued cautiously milling in place, hoping to remember the details to tell this story later as "drama on the high seas."

They would remember Khumalo making straight for one man, and people around that man widening their distance around him as she approached, until there was simply the two staring face to face.

For a wisp of a moment, he thought to go for the railing. The horizon, however, reminded him the ocean was as vast a space as any night sky. Instead, he tried to stand at his full height so he would appear taller than her.

He appeared smaller.

"You have been an unplucked thorn," he said.

"And you an annoyance beyond your station."

Sarantain drew his crossbow. Those watching drew even farther away, their sudden hubbub catching the captain's attention. He and several of his crew made way toward Khumalo, aft of the ship.

"Will your man kill me?" said the Thief Mage.

"Should you give him cause to."

"Cause," said Sarantain, "may be him blinking too fast, ma'am," his voice even and calm, aim unwavering.

"There are a hundred other ways for one such as yourself to feed," said Khumalo. "You chose otherwise. Your cohort could have remained unseen for ages. You chose otherwise."

"My husband," said Sarantain, "has spent more time healing the past days than in years at sea."

Twitswaddle glanced at Sarantain, then ignored him.

Sarantain drew the breath that came before firing but held it. Decided against it. Exhaled it away. "Captain Pinyasama," he called. "Shackles."

"I will not be bound as an animal," said Twitswaddle.

"Fortunately, you are being bound as a criminal," said Mother Khumalo. She turned away. Sarantain rounded behind the Thief

Mage, who wisely—and silently—followed Khumalo. Captain Malokofsky met them after a few paces, took in that all was as calm as one could hope, and nodded them on their way, he and his crew following them to the gangplank.

Khumalo crossed first. Twitswaddle and Sarantain second.

"May we never meet this way again," Malokofsky said to Maab.

"May there be fewer 'this ways' in all our days." She presented him a feather from her sarong. "Sail with honor."

He touched the feather to the brim of his blue captain's hat, returning the sentiment.

Pinyasama and her remaining crew left. The crew of the *Rest* untied the lashings and threw the rope over to the *Bane*'s waiting hands. The plank was raised and withdrawn. The two ships remained apart a moment as though regarding one another. Almost without being instructed to, sails on both ships quickly lowered. Rudders set to angle each ship away, and courses reset, one to see travelers, adventurers, laborers, and likely plunderers bound for new experiences, homes, and unsuspecting prey, the other for whatever semblance of order it could offer the small piece of the world awaiting it.

A tight-knit crowd gathered on the deck of the *Bane* to see what had been worth chasing a ship down as though the goddess herself had missed boarding. They saw a man who thought he was fancily dressed. In truth, nothing fit right. He tried to present an imperturbable air. What they saw made them wonder why they'd bothered coming out there.

He was a thing forgotten despite being in front of their eyes.

The old woman moved among that crowd, entirely unnoticed.

As she parted the front, Khumalo noticed.

Orsys looked older and frailer than Khumalo had ever beheld her. She looked more than tired; she looked resigned to fate, death, and sadness all at once. From an inner lining of the tatters she wore she pulled out a metallic cylinder filigreed with the image of a fiery dragoon, a cylinder with a bamboo handle grip. At not more than five paces away, she spat and aimed it at the Thief Mage.

After the sharp explosion, smoke, and instant chaos disappeared, Twitswaddle fell. Where his blanched forehead had been unblemished, there was a hole, color, and the sick air of singed flesh.

There was also Orsys, whose heart decided the noise and intent were more than it wanted to bear. She looked at Khumalo, her rheumy eyes already crying. "There's them as should not be alive," Orsys said, then closed her eyes. Her body crumpled.

Khumalo didn't move in time to catch her, but she was first to kneel in an attempt to stabilize the old woman with a proper flow of air. She ran a hand six inches over Orsys's body, then the same over Twitswaddle's. She returned to Orsys and whispered, "You were successful."

Pinyasama elbowed her way forward. "What in hells was that? What do we do now?"

Khumalo stood, tucking the cylinder in the sleeve of her robe. "Throw him overboard. Bring her to my quarters." She walked away from both bodies.

Stepple, of course, trailed after her.

When the two entered Khumalo's stateroom, no one could say what was done or said in there.

In the room she revealed the weapon.

"This's a new kind of magic, Madam. I purchased it at great discount from a man who said I gave the best massage of his entire life. Said he had an entire shipment en route to Waterfall. Said I could use this one as a sampler. We rode far on the beach during a storm, showed me all it could do. Told me to be precise with it and to never get it wet. Said so from beneath the biggest parasol I've ever seen. Red and white striped. I then told same to Orsys, who has always had the better hand."

"What ship are they on?"

"I thought you might need such. The *Bright Latch*. Due into harbor from Cekov in two weeks' time."

"Thank you."

"Put the fear of a witch into 'em," he said. The way said: a foregone command. "Folks don't need easier ways to die, need easier ways to live. Not everybody's killing wizards."

Khumalo opened the port on her wall and tossed the gun out.

"What can you do for Orsys?" Stepple beseeched.

"Nothing of benefit."

"Thought as such." He crossed to Khumalo, lip and body trembling, and dropped into her embrace. He hadn't known if she would catch him. Hadn't cared. He was tired of everything. One more fall wouldn't make a difference.

It mattered to Khumalo. She caught him without hesitation and let him cry into her. There was something to be said for being numb on occasion. After this, she might give it a try.

But right now, there were important things for her to feel.

"Madam, we have done unconscionable wrong," he sobbed.

Maab's crew knocked, then solemnly brought the body in, settling Orsys on the bed.

Khumalo gave Stepple space and ample time for numb shock to settle into each of his limbs. Quietly and equally solemnly, the crew exited to tend to their duties for the other body, that of a dead Thief Mage to be returned to Erah's waters for judgment.

Certain fish would likely find him tender.

Once Khumalo was assured of the well-being of the captain, crew, and Stepple Grandine, she made her farewells amidships on the fast vessel.

"Return swiftly and safely, and proceed the rest of your days with my full thanks," she said. She threw a portal. "I've never done this before."

"That'll get you home?"

"Yes?" Khumalo said, not entirely sure.

"Can you make a hole big enough for a boat?"

"There is another ship I'm hunting for. A weapons carrier. Perhaps we'll save that for then?"

"Agreed. I'll hunt with you in five days' time." Maab gave a look around at her ship, her crew. "We'll make for Waterfall at a slightly *subdued* pace."

"You are as wise as you are beautiful."

"I'll hold you to that sentiment."

***

A witch's story is only worth telling if she is changed by the end of it. This was on the first page of the little journal Mother Khumalo rarely showed anybody.

She stood on the docks of Waterfall. It was early morning. Far out to sea was a boat she had that very instant ported from.

She threw her head to the sky and whooped, not from happiness, certainly not victory. It was that she was that much nearer her daughter. She scared the gulls and stragglers who had yet to become used to seeing statuesque women in colorful clothing grace them from thin air.

With that same wild grin and a snap, she threw the portal to take her home.

LONG AFTER THAT

"**W**e stayed in Waterfall another two years," said Amnandi. It was best to tell one's own stories before others fashioned lies. "My friends became teachers themselves, of a sort. The village, to my knowledge, has only been attacked from within. Its citizenry. That is not a battle my mother or I will fight." Thus completed Amnandi's audience with the children. She glanced at the fire rather than add another log to it. After such a tale, their young minds were due a little magick. The waning flames resurged.

Khumalo limped into the room, readjusted the flame, and laid a heavy red shawl across Amnandi's back. She smiled at the children, touched the crown of each, then settled carefully on the floor beside them. "Live in a way that battles are unnecessary," she told them. She gave a single nod to her daughter to continue.

"Bog traveled. Tourmaline gained mastery when she taught

herself a spell on her own. Should you ever travel there, there are burials to visit to pay respects to. Speak their names in reverence. This history lesson is now over."

The four children stood, touched their foreheads to Balagon Amnandi and Witch Mother Khumalo, and exited the well-built home for the cold winter of Lerissa, a long ship's voyage along the southern horn of Eurola.

One child paused in the doorway. "Did you never go home?"

"We have many homes in different lands," said Amnandi, "but, yes, we have returned to Afrela many times."

The child shoved a knit cap over her springy hair. "I shall go next time." With that heavy pronouncement for such a young one, she pulled the door shut behind her. The chill wind swirled only a moment before respecting the warmth inside.

"I enjoy these sessions more than I imagined I would, Unina." Amnandi left her stool to sit hip to hip with her mother in front of the fire, spreading the shawl across both their shoulders. "You have word of Bog, don't you? I can tell from that smirk you're trying to hide."

"We have word of his location."

"His condition?"

"Well. How do you feel?"

"Unina...you cannot worry over me all your days."

"I have sufficient reserves."

"You never told me the last conversation you had with him," said Amnandi, looking as an adult so much like her mother that sometimes even spirits were confused.

Khumalo smiled. "We spoke about love."

"That seems appropriate."

"You've missed him, haven't you?"

"Very much."

"Had he stayed in Waterfall, he'd have stopped seeking certain things. As would we," Khumalo said. "He asked me:

"*Is this love, Khumalo?*'

"I laughed, saying, '*Would you like it to be love?*'

"'*I'm not sure I'm allotted,*' he said. A mischievous man.

"'*Define love,*' I asked.

"He answered immediately. '*An accumulation of kindnesses.*'

"'*It's not the worst definition.*'

"'*How does it fare against yours?*'"

At that, in the lodge with her daughter as winter breezes prowled among protection spells, Khumalo paused in remembrance. "I took his hand. Entwined his fingers. '*You don't need to know mine,*' said I. He prepared to raise our hands upward for a kiss. I pulled instead, letting my lips press for a moment against the coarse hairs and lattice of scars on his.

"I gave back his hand, knowing the warmth of my kiss lingered. '*Know* this.'

"'*Always,*' he agreed."

Amnandi caught the light in her mother's eyes. "Do we ride tonight?"

Khumalo snuggled closer and squeezed her daughter's forearm. "No. The fire is good. I wish to sit with you."

The woodsmoke was delicious. Crackles amid the hypnotic flames invited meditation. Both witches lost themselves in thoughts which were actually dreams which were actually universes—Amnandi's at times red, at times green, at times blue or black—both imagined Bog as an old man now, no, an old friend, and how good it would be to see him. The souls of friends, despite any amount of time or distance, were meant to be held. "*A witch knows,*" Unina had told Amnandi long before, "*it is warmth that matters.*"

"*And the only warmth that remains,*" young Amnandi had said, at which her mother kissed her forehead, blew out the candle lighting the small shack, and, as was Khumalo's favorite thing to do, comforted her child until their inhalations and exhalations matched one another, and both drifted softly to sleep.

**The Further Adventures of Mother Khumalo
and Amnandi continue in Book Two...**

AMNANDI SAILS

ACKNOWLEDGMENTS

Acknowledgments are the first magick of any boo[k]. They're where the inspiration, focus, and creative inte[rest] come from; the people, kindnesses, and outright lov[e] that get added like seeds to become a story.

Ma. Two small letters. One huge word.

Jasmine. Most Excellent Niece. If there's anybody who dream[s] bigger, they live on another plane of existence.

Cerece Rennie Murphy. A universe of inspiration.

Michael W. Lucas and Alex Kourvo, who've given me some of the greatest writerly wisdom possible: "Shut up and create!" from Michael; "Kiss your brain" from Alex. And more.

Beth Marshea. Literary champion.

Lesley Conner. The short story that introduced Mother Khumalo and daughter Amnandi a couple years back wouldn't have come about if not for her supreme baking skills and casually announcing, "The air in my house tastes like sugar!"

C.S.E. Cooney, who never fails to add wonder to my thoughts.

Beverly Jenkins, Patty Templeton, Jeffrey Ford, Robyn Bennis, and Richard Shealy for beta reads and edits above and beyond.

Jesse Hayes, whose art turns my books into paintings.

Every person who said yes to this book sight unseen.

Anna Tambour, for believing I can push boulders uphill.

And, as always, you.

Printed in the USA
CPSIA information can be obtained
at www.ICGtesting.com
LVHW050422280524
781480LV00003B/505

9 781732 298033